About the Author

Ted Winter studied Modern Languages at Manchester University and taught French, German and Spanish for 27 years before taking up writing. He had two A-Level study guides published before the lure of comic fiction proved irresistible. When not writing, he enjoys travelling, country walks and tennis. He lives in Dorset.

The Enigma of Four

Ted Winter

The Enigma of Four

Olympia Publishers
London

www.olympiapublishers.com
OLYMPIA PAPERBACK EDITION

A CIP catalogue record for this title is
available from the British Library.

ISBN: 978-1-78830-900-4

First Published in 2021

Olympia Publishers
Tallis House
2 Tallis Street
London
EC4Y 0AB

Printed in Great Britain

Dedication

To the self-sacrificing health care professionals around the world for their commitment and dedication during the Covid-19 lockdown of 2020.

Acknowledgements

I would like to thank my wife, Wendy, for giving me the nudge to follow my creative instincts in the first place and casting a critical but encouraging eye over the work. And all the teachers and children who have enriched my life over more than a quarter of a century and inspired me with ideas and an abundance of memories.

Chapter One
Along the Green Coast Line

Bear Hoskins gazed dreamily out of the carriage window at the leaden August sky. He reflected on his choice of holiday location and his decision to undertake the long day trip northwards to the Spanish border. Not for the first time in his solitary ventures, he asked himself whether he had made a mistake. The 'Costa Verde' was not known as the green coast for no reason. Whilst his contemporaries were basking in 30-degree warmth in the Algarve or the numerous better-known coasts of the Iberian Peninsula, Bear had elected to take his summer holiday in the far north-west of Portugal. True, the cruise along the Douro had been pleasant and he had persuaded himself that the historical sights of Porto had their worth, not least the visit to the Port wine lodge with the welcome accompanying samples. The three-day sojourn in Braga had embraced the energetic climb to the pilgrimage site of Bom-Jesus and the visit to Guimarães had more than satisfied his historical curiosity, enabling him to absorb the atmosphere of the site of Portugal's first kings. Yet as the dull, heavy sky continued to present a threatening accompaniment as his journey to the border town of Valença do Minho progressed, he began to wonder why he had insisted on this final outing.

Borders had always fascinated Bear since early

childhood. It was for this reason that he could not resist a train journey to the far north of Portugal and sneak into Spain, however briefly. He traced his passion inevitably to his numerous visits to relatives on his father's side to Carlisle and it had been a source of constant amusement to Bear and his siblings how his father had always proclaimed loudly on encountering the road sign the inscription, 'Welcome to Carlisle—The Great Border City'. Obligatory trips to Hadrian's Wall and occasional sorties into Scotland had reinforced in young Bear the fascination of being on the edge of the world, where one culture stopped and abruptly, adjustments had to be made as customs, signs, accents and shops took on a different hue on the other side, notwithstanding the ubiquitous multinational enterprises that seemed to seep into even the most rural of communities. Growing up as he had in suburban Surrey, the starkness of remote landscape, along with a testing local tongue to decipher from his aunts and uncles, presented a refreshing challenge to young Bear, entrenched as he was most of the year in the commuter belt and the stifling built-up environment.

He smiled to himself as memories flooded back to him of the recurrent leisure interest in his life. He had never been more animated than when following religiously the events of that tumultuous year of 1989 as that ultimate frontier—the Iron Curtain—was finally breached and hordes of ecstatic East Germans poured across Checkpoint Charlie to be embraced by West Berliners they had never seen. Bear had made a point on a previous holiday of visiting Berlin and other barren points along the old border between the two parts of Germany. His fascination with borders had reached ridiculous proportions when visiting a friend in Basel, Switzerland. When shown the famous 'Dreiländereck', the exact point in the Rhine where France, Germany and Switzerland meet, he had passed the camera to his host, dived into the river fully clothed to wave exuberantly from the precise spot where the countries were joined and ask his friend for a commemorative photo of the occasion. And borders had always been occasions for Bear. The photographic evidence in many cases had to be taken on trust as sometimes there was no sign that a new country was being entered, but this time it would be obvious, he anticipated, as the River Minho would definitely mark the end of Portugal and the beginning of Spain.

His reverie was abruptly halted by the French boy sitting on the opposite side of the carriage. As the train slowed down to enter one of the numerous stops on the route, the youngster, whom Bear guessed to be five or six years old, shot to his feet, gazed outside with bemusement and curiosity, and directed a mystified, almost accusing question at his mother, '*Pourquoi il s'arrête, le train*?' It was at this moment that Bear smiled to himself at his dim recollection of French classes that he had intermittently enjoyed but never put in the required effort to memorise. The woman's patient response was just decipherable, and in any case eminently guessable. Amidst reference to mounting and descending Bear deduced that the child was being informed that it was at such junctures that passengers got on and off. This lesson needed subsequent reinforcing as the identical questioning of the parent duly resumed at the next stop. Oh, to be five again, he reflected, to spend each day soaking in some facet of knowledge that makes just a little bit more sense of the world. He remembered the times playing with his niece and nephew, and his sister remarking on each visit that he was just a big kid at heart.

Angela's teasing of her younger brother had almost ritualistically included a reference to Bear's fascination with borders. Her repeated enquiries as to which frontier he intended to explore that year had started to be combined with speculation as to whether a future spouse would ever accompany her single sibling on such exploits. Bear's response was to smile, shrug his shoulders and to mumble something about having to follow one's passion. He was well aware that his family were eager to find out if he had found the lady of his dreams and he would finally 'settle down' and abandon his youthful zeal in favour of family life, but so far there had been no candidates for his affections and so borders were pursued with continued fervour.

The train resumed its grinding northward journey as the puzzled child opposite grudgingly accepted his mother's repeated explanation for the next scheduled stop. There was just one new passenger entering the carriage, a tall, dark, curly-haired young man with a pile of leaflets in his hand and carrying a satchel. A passable imitation of a 1970s footballer, mused Bear, half-speculating as to whether the newcomer might feign injury by colliding with the drinks trolley. The young man smiled benevolently at his fellow-travellers and approached Bear as his first customer. Having spent a week in the country and being used to having to fend off would-be salesmen with a *'Não falo português'*, Bear made the mistake of prefacing his stock response with a polite *'Desculpe'*, reasoning that he really ought to aspire to a certain level of linguistic proficiency after this time. Emboldened, his interlocutor sat opposite Bear on the edge of the facing seat and responded, *'Não faz mal'*, for some reason convinced that communication did not matter, and proceeded with a spiel from which Bear extracted the word *'criancas'* and assumed that the man wished to garner money for some children's cause. Why the man should think that a thirty-one-year-old history teacher from Suffolk should be likely to provide rich pickings was beyond Bear, who smiled vacantly and mumbled his incomprehension. His new companion, aware of a hopeless cause, promptly rose and looked elsewhere, turning briefly in the direction of the mother and son opposite. He decided, on reflection, against an approach on hearing French spoken with a slightly more irate tone, by the woman, presumably after yet another banal question from the child.

The rest of the journey passed without incident and the train drew into Valença do Minho station. Bear was left to reflect that, however colourless the rest of the day might prove, at least there were one or two amusing social interactions he could pass on to his colleagues and even pupils on his return to work in September.

Chapter Two
Border Encounter

Valença do Minho, at first glance, did not appear to have much to offer the typical tourist, especially on a dreary day in August. The museum seemed to be the only building beckoning curious travellers to linger and little in the way of amusements offered itself to divert the onlooker. As Bear bestrode the narrow streets and directed his steps towards the river and the frontier, the one thing that drew his attention was the market. It was a relatively small operation with a handful of stalls in a section of the street that had temporarily been pedestrianised, certainly not of the grandeur of some of the imposing market squares that adorn smaller towns throughout the continent of Europe. Yet there was a busyness about the place, an urgency to buy and sell, a sense of competitive vigour as if to take advantage of a rare opportunity that seemed striking. Surely, Bear asked himself, every market should be a hive of activity? Amidst the throng of customers, he was sure he could detect a change from nasal Portuguese consonants to the lisp of Spanish, and he realised that the town must be frequently visited by its Iberian neighbours in search of the latest bargain. Certainly, Portugal had a reputation for being inexpensive, and he had profited during his stay from reasonably priced accommodation, but it seemed that market day in Valença was a signal for a weekly invasion from across the border.

He carried on strolling through the town until he reached a point where the built-up area receded on one side and he was aware that he had alighted on to the river. Looking around, he saw solid banks of fortifications extending up the hillside on either side of the river, but more imposing in the town of Tui on the Spanish side, so it seemed. He headed down the street for a few hundred yards and came to the sight that arrested him, causing him to reach for his camera. The road veered off to his right and was replaced in view by a prominent iron bridge with a design not uncommon for the latter part of the nineteenth century. Bear carefully removed his camera from its case and took three photos, all of which ensured the bridge had pride of place but also that part of the fortifications on the Spanish side were in view. Above all, it had to be clear that he had arrived at a border. As he approached the bridge, he sought out the commemorative plaque that confirmed that Gustave Eiffel was the engineer responsible for linking the two countries, with a more obviously practical project than his famous tower.

The urge to photograph was not just a result of Bear's passion for borders. He knew that he would not feel able to set foot in the staff room of Princewood School, Suffolk, unless he were able to supply photographic evidence of his exploits. Not that he felt the need to prove where he had been, but almost by accident, he had got into the habit of passing on holiday photos of borders to one of his colleagues. Rachel Rhodes taught geography at the school. She had joined the staff one year after Bear, and in a chance conversation at the end of her first year, Bear had revealed that he was visiting the Pyrenees, with a view to crossing over from Spain to France.

Bear had casually offered to supply Rachel with pictures of an exact point where one country becomes another as if to prove his fascination with frontiers. She had said that any up-to-date pictorial references to the physical border would greatly help reinforce the clarity of the displays in her classroom. As a result, Bear had returned with the desired images, which were gratefully received, and in the two summer holidays that followed, he had provided Rachel with further representations that had enhanced the visual appeal of her surroundings. It was a source of amusement to Bear, and a challenge to him to secure the clearest, sharpest images of border points for his colleague ever since. Hence the care with which he took the photos of the bridge and the riverbanks on this occasion.

After crossing into Spain, Bear followed the road that led uphill into what he presumed was the centre of Tui. An imposing church had been visible from the Portuguese side and he naturally decided that this edifice would be a magnet for tourists. As he made his way up the street, he could not help noticing that the town centre of Tui was much quieter than its counterpart on the other side of the Minho. His suspicions that market day, and the favourable Portuguese currency, meant that trading was much less feverish north of the border, were confirmed. He mused as to what effect the proposed introduction of a single currency across much of the European Union would have on cross-border business.

His thoughts returned to the photos he had taken. He knew Rachel would be pleased with his efforts, whatever their quality. She had a bubbly, sanguine temperament, seemingly always ready to be the life and soul of any party, and effusive in her appreciation for anything done for her. Bear recalled the first occasion, three Septembers ago, when he had provided the initial set of border photos for his colleague. He had taken a late summer holiday that year, and as a result the photos had not been developed until the first week of the autumn term. Having transferred the images neatly into a brown envelope, he intended to give them to Rachel at breaktime but, on an impulse, decided to take a detour via her classroom. As the history and geography classrooms were located in the same block, he did not have to go far out of his way. Noticing her classroom was open, he half-knocked, entered and saw that Rachel was in light-hearted discussion with two pupils, a boy and a girl of about fifteen from a Year 11 class. Bear had briefly smiled, placed the envelope on Rachel's desk with a conjuror's sleight of hand and said,

'Present for you. Sorry to disturb.'

'Thank you very much,' Rachel responded warmly. 'That's most kind.'

'A present?' The girl had echoed with curiosity.

'Is it your birthday, miss?' The boy had probed further.

Bear had already exited the room in pursuit of his mid-morning coffee and had not caught Rachel's response. It had transpired that, whatever she had said, far from repelling the pupils' inquisitiveness, merely inflamed it. The rumour mill in Year 11 had soon sprung into life with the prominent headline that 'Mr Hoskins is going out with Miss Rhodes'. It had taken most of that academic year for these fires to be extinguished. Fortunately, some of the students had moved on at the end of the year, and those who returned for A-Levels were consumed with more scintillating topics of gossip. However, Bear had been made acutely aware, as if he needed to be, that his actions are constantly scrutinised by the student population.

Mildly berating himself for allowing thoughts of school

and the return to the daily grind of work to cloud his holiday mood, Bear realised he had reached the church he had observed earlier. Scanning the notice boards in front of the building, Bear was able to ascertain that the church was, in fact, a cathedral, the Catholic cathedral, constructed in the 13th century and offering a blend of Romanesque and Gothic architecture. He duly stepped inside to admire the quality of workmanship and gather his thoughts. Enjoying the curious sensation common to many cathedrals and large churches, of a sense of boundless space with distant vaulted ceilings but often tempered by limited lighting that suggested restricted room, Bear sat down on one of the pews and admired the various scenes from the stained-glass windows. His acquaintance with Latin enabled him to follow some of the Biblical stories depicted where the images were obscure. After twenty minutes wandering through the cathedral, he tried unsuccessfully to decipher the contents of information boards, solely in Spanish, but gave up after he recognised little more than the centuries in which events took place. How unusual it was, he reflected, in this day and age, not to be supplied with an English translation. How fascinating and reassuring, he mused further, that there are still places so out of the way that they are not desperate to pander to the needs of the compulsive tourist.

Bear felt a sense of fulfilment, as he often did, at having crossed a border and made comparisons between the surroundings on each side of the divide. The historian in him persuaded him to make the effort to research the background of the Luso-Spanish frontier, and how he could throw that experience into future lessons. That, however, was a project for later. Feeling sated with his amble through the centre of

Tui, he decided, perhaps still intrigued by the more frenzied market atmosphere in Valença, that he would spend the rest of the afternoon on the Portuguese side. Half an hour later, after a half-hearted browse through a couple of souvenir shops, he alighted upon a café with three or four tables outside on the pavement. He selected a seat at an empty table and when a waitress approached, carefully articulated his by now well-practised line, *'Un galão, por favor'*. Congratulating himself that one of his targeted Portuguese phrases had found its mark, he opened his tourist guide to check for any remaining must-see sights that were within reach before the end of his stay. The waitress returned with his milky coffee and he settled himself to consult the guidebook for one of the last times before returning home.

Perhaps because Bear had been distracted by the constant reminders to encourage the reader to refer to the end of the guidebook, he had started to become engrossed in the history of Portugal. He was just reading a lengthy section explaining the importance of the Restoration in the 17th century and its relevance to certain sights around the country when he realised that the clouds had darkened considerably. Never one to be caught out, Bear took his half-drunk galão, (he was happy to drink coffee lukewarm in the summer) inside the café, where there were only four tables, along with half a dozen bar stools. He repositioned himself at one of the tables. The expected downpour, when it came, was torrential. Within seconds several people who had been surveying the market stalls decided to take cover in the café, immediately occupying chairs at the other tables and a few of the bar stools. Two of the newcomers reasoned that it was only right and proper to make a purchase and approached the bar to order drinks. A minute later another new customer entered. Pulling off the hood of a dark blue cagoul, a young woman, perhaps in her late twenties, dressed casually in faded blue jeans and a white polo-necked sweater, smiled and blew out through her cheeks in a visible expression of relief at having escaped the rain. She surveyed her surroundings in search of a seat. By now every table was at least partly occupied, but at Bear's table two seats were still vacant.

Bear was vaguely aware of the question in one Iberian language or another that was directed to him, but it was obvious from the context that the new arrival was asking if Bear objected to her occupying any of the vacant seats at his table. He indicated with a quiet smile that he had no objection, and she sat down in the seat adjacent to him with her back to the rain, as if totally unconcerned about a possible lengthy delay before returning outside. She took off her cagoul and draped it on the back of the chair. Bear observed her out of the corner of his eye, thinking that this was someone who was very much at ease with her surroundings. It was a few minutes before the waitress was able to come around to take her order as she had been engaged with attending to the sudden influx of requests at the bar. The young woman asked for a blackcurrant tea and waited calmly as Bear buried himself in his guidebook. When the drink arrived, she allowed her teabag to remain in the cup for a while before asking Bear a question, presumably in Portuguese. She seemed to be gesturing to an object on the table near Bear, but all he could respond with was a nervous smile and a puzzled look. Then it dawned on him that she was asking for the ash tray, not for the purposes of smoking, but to place her discarded teabag on. Bear slid the ash tray over, saying,

'Sorry… I mean, *"desculpe".*'

'That's okay,' she replied, adding, 'You must be English?'

'Is it that obvious?'

'A bit of an obvious clue from the title of your book,' Bear's new table companion replied, carefully squeezing the teabag of remaining liquid and depositing it on the ashtray, while Bear closed the book to reveal: *Portugal—The Essential Guide.*

Bear smiled, as much bemused as startled that someone could spot the small print of the book's sub-title. The country's name, of course, was spelt identically in several languages, but it would have taken a sharp eye to decipher any accompanying text. It seemed the woman detected Bear's surprise, so, in order to avert any unnecessary question, added,

'Sorry, it's force of habit. I work in books, and I've seen that series before. The cover design and lettering colour is quite distinctive.'

'You're in publishing? Travel books?' Bear enquired, grateful of the opportunity to develop some conversation on what was proving a rainy afternoon.

'No, I'd like to get into travel,' his companion answered, 'but I'm in education publishing at the moment, selling books to schools.'

Bear had adopted the habit on holiday of making the most of the opportunity of being in the 'real' world, away from education, and on a few memorable occasions when he struck up conversation with a stranger, was able to congratulate himself on not revealing his profession until absolutely necessary. He found that if he shared that he was a teacher straight away, he would inevitably but unwittingly draw his interlocutor into a conversation about the decline in discipline or standards in schools, or smart comments about the length of holidays he was lucky enough to enjoy. He found it rewarding to move away from topics related to the classroom and would lead the discussion to any avenue that took his fancy. In more than one instance, when he was compelled to disclose his occupation after a lengthy chat, he remembered with fondness that his new acquaintance had remarked, 'I would never have thought you were a teacher', or 'I had you down as…' This occasion on a gloomy afternoon in northern Portugal was not one of those instances, and Sophie Bingham was to prove to be no ordinary acquaintance.

So began by far the longest conversation Bear had experienced during his stay in Portugal. The rain showed no sign of relenting, and what seemed an unspoken agreement between two compatriots abroad determined that it was in each of their interests to develop some degree of entertaining chat, if possible, for the time that they were confined. Sophie was quite direct in her questioning, as Bear was later to experience regularly, and asked him what he did for a living. She was incredulous that even a teacher would find anything vaguely fulfilling in venturing to this isolated region, to which Bear replied that he was intrigued by the differences between the two countries and felt the urge to visit Spain on this trip. He felt he would rather not launch into his passion for borders at this early stage of conversation as he needed to be sure his companion could handle such an unorthodox interest.

Discussion soon turned to Sophie's reason for being in the region.

'My dad and his partner run a riding stables in Galicia, about twenty miles north of Tui. I'm just here on a short visit.'

She did not elaborate on her experiences, and Bear had the

distinct impression that Sophie was not on the warmest terms with the two aforementioned people, and that she had decided to visit as a duty, in ticking a necessary but unwelcome box in her calendar. She did add, though, that she had earmarked that day for a visit over the border to Valença market to see if she could pick up any bargains. Bear asked her if she had been successful in her quest.

'I bought a few things. A couple of tops, and a set of three scarfs. I managed to get the price knocked down by twenty escudos,' she said with her salesperson's satisfaction at seeing her strategy bear fruit. She reached into a plastic shopping bag to show Bear the three scarves, still in their transparent wrapper, of different colours, each with a distinct floral design. 'Oh, and this…'

Sophie reached further into her bag and produced a bronze brooch and placed it on the table. At first glance, there was nothing remarkable about the piece of jewellery. Bear was about to mutter some non-committal, polite appreciation of her choice when his eyes started to focus on some of the detail. Although the brooch was no more than two inches tall and fractionally smaller in width, the intricacy of the craftsmanship was certainly impressive. In the centre was a figure of a horseman with folds in his clothing clearly visible. He was carrying what seemed like a lance, as though embarking on a medieval tournament. In the background the artisan had created delicate ridges that at first sight looked like waves but were more probably indicative of flames. From Bear's brief acquaintance with Sophie, he deduced that it was her love of horses that had been a major motivation for the purchase, and she confirmed that this was so. Around the exterior of the image was a ring with what seemed like a coat of arms to the left and a similar insignia on the right, with a Latin inscription in the middle. Bear was no antiques expert but could appreciate the skill that had been applied in creating the ornament. Probably, he concluded, the supposedly inferior quality metal had enabled Sophie to make the transaction at a reasonable price.

'It's a very nice design, and well preserved, by the look of things,' he commented. 'Do you know how old it is?'

'I think the guy said it was nineteenth century, but I'm not that bothered. I just like the design. What does that motto say—something about being strong united?'

'*Unita fortior*,' Bear read aloud. 'It means strong*er* united. I suppose there's a story behind that, somewhere.' Little did he know how he would be left to reminisce about the enormity of the understatement of this remark.

The rain continued unabated, and Bear was in no hurry to brave the downpour. He knew he had at least an hour and a half before the next train south and was quite happy for the conversation to pursue some predictable paths. Not for the first time, Bear found himself more in the role of listener. Some of his colleagues had wondered if he had ever undergone training as a counsellor (he hadn't), as he was able to allow people to maintain a lengthy, often tedious monologue, without interrupting. Bear was also very adroit in selecting the right question to ask, and often his well-timed contribution had been just what his companion had needed to hear and had been grateful for his insight. This pattern was developing now with Sophie. Bear asked a few questions which enabled Sophie to open up about her passion for riding, her job, her parents' divorce and the occasional visits to rural Spain which she endured, punctuated by being able to ride and pursue bargains over the border. Bear was conscious that he was in danger of giving the impression of probing too far and too intrusively, and more than once prefaced his question with an apologetic, 'If you don't mind me asking...'

Sophie, in fact, was more than happy to be interrogated. Like Bear, she had enjoyed little meaningful conversation over the past week and was genuinely interested in thinking through issues Bear raised. What a change for a bloke to ask my opinions and feelings on certain matters, she reflected. In her job she was well versed in fielding queries from customers and responding with a pre-planned sales line. It was a pleasure to begin to articulate her motivation in an unthreatening environment. As she relaxed more, she felt even able to share some anecdotes about colleagues she did not always get on with. Why not, she asked herself, I'll probably never see this chap again, I can let off a bit of steam about the odd grievance without fear of recriminations.

Bear responded in kind with a few observations of colleagues, albeit more reserved, and more complimentary. He too felt more at ease as what had seemed to be verging on cross-examination was favourably received. In fact, he had established a bit of a reputation at school for his questioning technique. Conscious of the diversity of temperaments represented in the average classroom, he had over the years developed a range of questions to stimulate debate on historical issues. He was just as adept at 'What would you have done...?' questions that challenged the more confident students who were outspoken at some ruler's misguided policy, as he was in issuing a 'What would you have thought if...?' reflection, inviting the quieter pupils to participate by putting them in the shoes of citizens suffering under a despotic regime. He was not averse to an appeal to the emotions; his 'How would you have felt if...?' questions had stimulated some impassioned break-time arguments over the years. Most famously, his tantalising, end-of-lesson posers that were left to hang in the air, seemed to be immaculately timed to preclude any debate until the next lesson, deliberately designed to give his students three days to think over the issue. Sometimes, of course, the question was forgotten by the time they reconvened, but more often than not, the extra thinking time had produced a range of well-rehearsed views that had ignited the topic they were studying.

Conversation turned naturally to their respective interests, travels they had each made and where they lived. Sophie had moved to Camden in north London two years previously when she took up her current position with a publisher's and was intrigued to know about Suffolk, a region she had not encountered before. Briefly Bear found himself in the role of speaker rather than listener. They each ordered further drinks as the afternoon wore on. They observed that they were not the only ones seeing out the storm in the café. Having finished her second blackcurrant tea, Sophie suddenly glanced at her watch.

'My goodness, is that the time? I'm sorry, I've got to fly. Last bus leaves Tui in twenty-five minutes,' she remarked with alarm, hastily gathering her purchases together, much to the amusement of Bear who had spent several years keeping a close eye on the time, carefully dividing each lesson into time segments so as not to overrun, unless a healthy debate was in full swing.

'It's been nice to meet you, Bear. Maybe see you again some time.'

Bear uttered a pleasantry about Sophie's work bringing her to Suffolk one day, and she hurriedly left a note to cover her two drinks for Bear to settle the bill. With that she left the café and prepared for what would be a brisk run down to the bridge and back over the border to catch her bus. Bear consulted his watch, realised he could afford to stay in the café for another half-hour or so before returning to the station and settled down again to return to his guide. It was after a few minutes that a growing sense of unease crept over him. He looked up from his book to notice, with a sense of awkwardness and horror, that the bronze brooch was still lying on the table where Sophie had showed it to him two hours earlier.

Chapter Three
New Term at Princewood

The dry spell at the end of August had shown no signs of abating, and Rob McAllister had been coming to terms with an uncomfortable truth. The ground at Princewood School's playing fields had hardened so much over the summer that there was a distinct possibility that the forthcoming rugby season would have to be delayed, with fixtures cancelled. Players' safety was the paramount concern, and if heavy tackles on a bone-hard surface were likely to result in injuries, alternative physical education options would have to be pursued. To most staff at the school, any such rearrangement was of tangential, if any, significance. To Rob, however, the postponement of September fixtures was a cause of grave concern. His Under-16 team had been hailed as the most promising group for years, and he had been looking forward to working with them as their coach. In particular, he had been eagerly awaiting the early weeks of the season, with several winnable fixtures awaiting. The dry grounds looked like putting paid to the expected dream start until the much-appreciated downpours of the first weekend in September, just before term was due to begin. As he drove into the school grounds that Monday morning for the staff meeting and training day, he was anxious to ascertain whether the rains had softened the ground sufficiently.

As he stepped out of his Mazda MX-5 Miata, Rob noticed two figures in earnest discussion at the edge of the rugby pitch adjacent to the car park. He guessed immediately the topic of their conversation and was proved right.

'Morning, gents, what's the lie of the land?' he asked.

'Morning, Rob,' Head of Games Stuart Prentice replied, and the head groundsman added his greeting. 'Fred reckons we might be all right by the weekend.'

'So long as we don't get another heatwave,' cautioned Fred Wheeler. 'There's more rain forecast for later in the week, and the ground should be soft enough by then.'

'That's fine, isn't it, Stu? We wouldn't be doing full contact this first week anyway,' responded Rob, relieved. He trusted Fred's considerable experience on meteorological matters and even Suffolk's reputation as England's driest county was unlikely to thwart his sporting ambitions for the season.

'Sounds good,' agreed Stuart. 'Thanks, Fred,' he added, turning to move back to the main school buildings, 'See you at the games meeting, if not before, Rob.'

Rob was left at the edge of the pitch with the head groundsman for a moment. The playing fields were in immaculate condition. They both knew, of course, that by mid-November the fields would have cut up and grass would be replaced by mud, but the pristine turf seemed to transmit a pleasing aroma of new beginnings that was worth savouring. Rob was happy to linger and survey the scene. He savoured the fresh warm air with the relish of a busy chef, tasting one of his delicious creations in a rare moment of calm before the storm of the restaurant's demands returned. He knew that he had to head indoors shortly for a demanding day of meetings.

First, the staff meeting, chaired by the headmaster, in which examination results were dissected with surgical precision. With English being a core subject, Rob's department was naturally under the spotlight each year, but he was relieved that his pupils had avoided some of the worst-case scenarios he had envisaged, and there had been a few pleasant surprises of candidates just making the grade that they were striving for. Like many of his colleagues, Rob often reflected, results day in August was 'the best of times, the worst of times'.

After a few moments of amiable chat, during which they exchanged details of holidays and discussed prospects of sports teams, speculated about new members of staff and how recently departed staff were getting on in pastures new, Fred waited patiently for the inevitable question. It was like a pre-term ritual with certain teachers. Rob duly obliged.

'So, what have you got for me this time, Fred?'

Anyone listening in to snatches of their conversation would have assumed Fred was dealing in drugs. In fact, the 63-year-old groundsman's passion was horses. He had been working at Princewood for nearly thirty years, from the time it was still the town's boys' grammar school before becoming mixed and marketing itself as 'the leading co-educational independent school in East Suffolk'. With promotion to Head Groundsman soon following after a few years, he was fortunate to have a house that went with the job, on the edge of the school grounds. Consequently, he had no rent to pay, which was just as well, as he was periodically in debt after he had backed yet another loser. To be fair, he was a reasonable judge of form and had enjoyed enough success in gambling to stay afloat and strive for the one big payday that never came.

'Nice looking filly running in the 2.30 at Musselburgh.

Tango Queen. You could do worse—decent odds, fifteen to one.'

'Hmm,' mused Rob. 'Anything on the Saint Leger?'

'Touch and go. Depends on the going. There's been more rain up north, and if it's too soft one of my tips may be pulled out. We'll just have to wait and see.'

Rob thanked Fred for his tip and headed to the school hall, where the first of a series of meetings was due to commence. After the results post-mortem and introduction of new staff, of which there were three this year, general school business was to be presented by the Head, Stephen Rawlinson, supported by contributions by his deputies, Angela Banks and David Wilkinson. After a break for coffee a training session had been arranged with a visiting speaker, followed by department meetings after lunch. Finally, Stuart's games meeting was scheduled for 4.00 p.m. Rob mentally geared himself for information overload.

He was not alone in preparing himself for the onslaught. Bear had enjoyed a leisurely last fortnight of the holidays but there had been a lingering sense of disquiet bordering on disbelief at the predicament he had been left in by Sophie's sudden dash for the bus in Portugal and finding himself the unwilling custodian of what looked like quite an attractive piece of jewellery. As he took his seat in the third row of seating at the school hall, waiting for proceedings to begin, he reflected again on the improbability of the turn of events and the fact that he had as yet done nothing about it. How had he failed to spot the brooch on the table until too late? Of course, he had thought of running after Sophie and intercepting her before the bus had departed, but not even his zeal for traversing frontiers could counteract the sound reasoning that a third border crossing that day would be futile. By the time he had noticed the problem, some twenty minutes had elapsed, by which time Sophie would either have boarded the bus or, less likely, returned to the café, having registered the lack of a brooch and resigned herself to spending the night in one of the border towns. He had decided to stay put in the café and hope to see Sophie burst in to reclaim her purchase, but quickly realised this was not going to happen. He thought of handing it in to the café owners but dismissed this course of action immediately: for one thing, his Portuguese was not up to explaining his predicament coherently; for another, he was not at all confident that Sophie would look in this establishment. She might not remember where she had mislaid her brooch, and in any case, with relations cool between herself and her father and his partner, was she likely to make a return visit to the region any time soon? Bear was left with an unwanted piece of luggage as he returned to England two days later, with a resolve to try to return the brooch to its owner.

These thoughts had assailed Bear for the rest of that rainy afternoon and returned to him as he half-heartedly scanned the minutes of the staff meeting that was about to take place. Could he have done more to contact her in the fortnight since flying home? The past two weeks had seen him busy preparing for the beginning of term. He had been into school a couple of times, once for results day and a second time to tidy up his classroom and open his annual stationery order, ready to distribute exercise books and paper once classes began. He had been into London for one of his occasional visits to the city's bookshops and had slipped into a library to consult the yellow telephone directory to scan the section 'Publishers'. It quickly became apparent that he was looking for a needle in a haystack, or, as his witty Head of Department Michael Streatham once remarked, 'You've got to find the right haystack first.' There was no section in the yellow pages on 'Educational Publishers' and a long list of some three hundred companies yielded few clues as to Sophie's probable employers. This is ridiculous, Bear told himself: we spent over two hours in each other's company, and we didn't find out the names of our respective employers. Bear was certain he hadn't divulged the name of Princewood School—otherwise by now one of the school secretaries would have contacted him to say there was a young lady from such-and-such a publishing company wishing to speak to him. In years to come, Bear would reflect on the absurdity of his hapless search as a few short clicks of the mouse would have narrowed down the likely places of employment of someone called Sophie, Sales Representative, but regular engagement with the world-wide web was still a few years away. He resigned himself to abandoning his investigations until such time as he came up with a better idea, which was not forthcoming as he prepared to face the challenges of the new academic year.

He was abruptly awoken from his reverie by Rob McAllister thumping down his massive frame in the seat next to him.

'How's it going, Bear?'

'Not so bad, Mac. I wasn't sure I would see you at this unholy hour after last night's session.'

'You know me, Bear. Play hard, work hard. Always on time.'

Bear smiled quietly, raising both eyebrows. There was certainly no doubting the first half of his friend's motto, as the previous evening had indicated. The Anchor Inn, just off market square in the centre of town, was one of a dying number of old-fashioned pubs that had resisted the trend toward converting to a restaurant. It remained fundamentally a drinking establishment where the only food served were peanuts and crisps. It provided a convivial atmosphere, with attractive nineteenth-century wooden furnishings and bookshelves lined with hardback novels from the 1930s, designed to create an ambiance of definitely not moving with the times. The Anchor, more significantly, was known as the teachers' pub. Whilst it was widely acknowledged that under-age drinking took place, Princewood School pupils knew very well that The Anchor was off-limits and was the favoured watering hole of their teachers at the weekends. It had also been the tradition among many of the staff to spend their last night of freedom at The Anchor Inn before the autumn term began. Until recently about fifteen to twenty colleagues had assembled at the local hostelry at the end of the staff training day and the eve of term proper, but it had been moved back a day as many had voted with their feet, favouring abstinence and a good night's sleep after a demanding day of meetings and paperwork. Sunday night, the eve of the training day, had become the chosen option. Hardened party animals such as Rob had wondered why the need for a change. The previous evening in The Anchor had been a jovial occasion; all three new members of staff had attended, eager to be seen to be fostering the convivial spirit. Bear had enjoyed engaging in conversation with two of them, as well as meeting up with colleagues he had not seen over the summer. When he had taken his leave at just after ten, electing to pursue the long walk to the other side of the riverside town of Princewood, his friend Rob had already consumed four pints and was in heated discussion with a couple of colleagues. Not on any of the finer points of European literature, as one might have surmised, but on the laws of rugby union which had recently been amended to facilitate more open play. Alan Cartwright, Modern Languages teacher in his mid-forties, delighted in clearing up little linguistic conundrums about case endings and transitive or intransitive verbs. He also loved sorting sporting disputes out succinctly, especially refereeing decisions, with the alacrity of an overenthusiastic quiz show contestant. He saw himself as something of a refereeing expert and it was not unknown for a full-blown debate to break out on some topic of officiating, fuelled by an anecdote or two of an arbiter's error influencing the result of a contest otherwise long since forgotten. Such a lengthy exchange of views had engrossed Alan and Rob. Realising he was unlikely to get a look in for a long time, Bear had decided to take his leave, half-expecting to see Rob the worse for wear after a long evening.

For the past two years Bear had enjoyed a warm friendship and amicable working relationship with Rob. They had been paired together to run the Under-16 rugby teams. There was only a year between them, Rob having turned 32 over the summer, but they were very different in physique. Rob was tall, six foot three, a thoroughly athletic, broad-framed all-round sportsman who opened the bowling for Wanderswick village team on Sundays during the summer and had played a major role in the club's progress to a national final two summers back. He was genuinely knowledgeable on a range of sports as much as he was about English literature, and he communicated his enthusiasm to his charges passionately. Bear, of medium height and weight, was quite happy to serve as his deputy in running the understudy team of that year group. He cheerfully accepted that the senior partner could plunder the B-team for talent when injuries arose and was happy with the arrangement that allowed him some free Saturdays during the rugby term, as not all opponents could field second-string sides for fixtures. Bear tended to leave the complex training drills to Rob, content to run through some basic moves prior to match day. Winning was far from everything for Bear, but he had succeeded over the years in putting on a bit of a front, acquiring a few motivational phrases of his own. The pair came across as an effective double act and Bear was known as a calming influence on his colleague. This quality had been much in evidence after Rob had to be calmed down after struggling to control his fury at a perceived refereeing injustice but was not confined to the sports field. Bear recalled how, about eighteen months previously, his friend had called on him late one evening fighting off tears after his then girlfriend had broken with him. She had found him 'too intense', Rob had related, bewildered. Bear couldn't disagree with her assessment but maintained a dignified silence. This occasion with Rob had been one of a few in which Bear's growing reputation as a counsellor had emerged.

The pair had just enough time to exchange details of their respective holidays before the meeting opened. Rob had barely elicited from Bear that the latter had spent a rainy day in the last café in Portugal before launching into his dialogue with Alan the night before and Bear was unaware of Rob's latest holiday movements. He enquired.

'Côte d'Azur, mate,' replied Rob. 'Can thoroughly recommend it, for a variety of reasons.'

'I take it one of the reasons might have something to do with female company?' Bear probed. For anyone else, such an enquiry might have been deemed cheeky, but Bear knew his friend's reputation as a ladies' man so well (and Rob knew that he knew) that it was a formality that the answer would be in the affirmative.

'Affirmative. You can say that again,' replied Rob with a wink.

'I'd rather not, but I'm sure you'll elaborate in due course.'

'All in good time, dear boy.'

The conversation was cut short as Stephen Rawlinson took his seat at the centre of the long table facing the audience, indicating proceedings were due to begin. There was just time for Alan Cartwright to greet Rob in passing, whispering, 'Depends on whether the ref was playing advantage.' He gave Rob a playful but challenging look before sitting down, congratulating himself that what he had apparently been wrestling over since closing time had reached a satisfying conclusion.

The meeting opened with a welcome back to all colleagues from the headmaster, and a welcome to the three new members of staff. He drew the attention of all present to various papers placed on their seats, starting with a results summary for public examinations. The A-Level results had, he noted, exceeded expectations, for which he congratulated the teachers for their hard work during the previous year, but the GCSE results were disappointing in places. 'To aspire to the status of the leading independent school in the region, we need to get as many pupils into the "promised land" as possible, meaning all the way through to university offers and places. But,' he emphasised, 'they can't get to the promised land if they're stuck in the desert and not enough are getting the

GCSE grades to want to stay on beyond 16.' Grounds for optimism, but no room for complacency was the message. The headmaster added further news on development of the site, special needs programmes, the establishment of a curriculum committee to discuss matters such as a change to an earlier choice of option subjects being mooted, and safeguarding issues.

The deputies added additional items on communication channels, pastoral concerns and the need for judicious choice in suggesting trips out of school, with due notice advised for such ventures. There was nothing out of the ordinary, although plenty of detail to take in. Over coffee Bear took advantage of the opportunity to present Rachel with her photos. He didn't dare risk a repeat of the embarrassment of three years ago by making the transfer in front of any children. He was particularly pleased at how they had come out, with even the lettering on the Eiffel plaque clearly legible, and Rachel was suitably impressed and effusive in her thanks. I could emulate such warm-hearted gratitude, thought Bear. He considered making a new year resolution (September being the start of the new year for all teachers) to be warmer in his expression of gratitude, realising how appreciated he felt by Rachel's response.

His thoughts were cut short by a familiar shrill Gallic voice addressing him. 'So, 'ow eez my grizzly Bear? 'ow was your summer?'

'Very good, thanks, Claudine. Usual stuff, you know— played a bit of tennis, caught up with friends and family, a bit of walking in the hills, couple of weeks in Portugal.' Bear congratulated himself on this succinct description, a quality he was constantly trying to encourage in his pupils.

'I don't believe eet for a moment. With you, Bear, nothing eez usual. Your life eez one great adventure of discovery and passion.'

Claudine Leblanc, of all the teachers at Princewood School, was the most fascinated by Bear's sustained passion for borders and how they influenced cultures. A handsome, immaculately dressed woman in her mid-forties, she had been teaching French at the school for some eight years and had lost little of her Gallic flamboyance since moving to England from Bordeaux in her late twenties. Initially, she had acquired a slightly unfair reputation as a teacher more concerned with style than precision and would often encourage pupils to express themselves freely, whether orally or in writing, at the expense of grammatical accuracy. Fears that her approach would have an adverse effect on students' results, however, were proved unfounded, and her groups regularly secured high grades at all levels. She had seemed to have got over her acrimonious divorce six years earlier and showed no inclination to return to France. It was noted that she naturally leaned more toward conversation with her male colleagues than with the female staff, and Bear had initially felt uneasy that Claudine might have an interest in mothering him, or even seeking an intimate relationship. As the years passed, it was clear that she had no such designs, but she was curiously stimulated by anyone's unusual interests, and was constantly urging Bear to follow his passion, and was always keen to learn about which border he had crossed.

Bear tried to deflect Claudine's questioning with small talk.

'So how was your holiday, Claudine? Did you get back to France at all?'

'Briefly, but I was mainly in Italy on Lake Como. Eet was wonderful. But tell me about your 'oliday.'

As anticipated, Bear's attempt to play down the significance of his recent trip failed. It was not as if he wanted to dismiss his visit to Portugal as insignificant or not memorable, as he had enjoyed many aspects of his stay. He just knew that even relating a relatively mundane experience would draw an exaggerated reaction from Claudine which would cause her either to exclaim in audible astonishment or to burst into unexpected and sustained laughter. Bear knew there was always a danger of colleagues engaged in quieter conversations turning around to observe that the two of them were getting on 'like a house on fire'. The trouble was that the more he tried to adopt a deadpan face and relate an experience as commonplace or at best, mildly unusual, the more Claudine would spot something fascinating and wish to pursue some unspoken, hidden adventure that she was determined to draw from him.

So it was that Bear spent most of the twenty minutes of the coffee break telling Claudine all about the day's visit to Valença and inevitably, because Claudine was so probing, his encounter with Sophie was included. He was relieved that the break was drawing to a close just at the point where he would have had to think of a way to avoid talking about the brooch. He was still wondering how he could return it to its owner and didn't want anyone, especially one as inquisitive as Claudine, to know that he was the involuntary guardian of someone else's property. Claudine made as to return to her seat with a pat on the shoulder and a knowing look. 'You must follow your passion. Maybe you will meet 'er again, zis Sophie.'

'Who knows?' Bear replied in a non-committal fashion. 'I

look forward to hearing more about Lake Como,' he added as they resumed their seats.

The rest of the day proved stimulating at times, if inevitably tiring. The guest speaker for the training session, Dr Pamela Simpson of the CanDo Foundation, represented a government-funded organisation devoted to using affirmative language and action to boost insecure children and maximise their potential. When the headmaster introduced the guest and explained the nature of her work and the likely direction of her talk, there was a slightly exasperated intake of breath by some, but also some interested raised eyebrows in other quarters. If anyone had been in a position to notice, it would have been apparent that the reaction was broadly divided according to age. Michael Streatham, Bear's Head of Department, a balding man in his mid-fifties with prominent thick eyebrows and a piercing stare, sitting along the row from him, muttered to himself, 'What a waste of time. Teaching grandmothers to suck eggs.'

Some of the longer-standing colleagues seemed to be of similar opinion. However, there were supportive smiles from the younger members of staff, and it was noticeable that once the gathering was divided into groups to discuss case studies, most teachers were warming to the task and participating freely. Dr Simpson was ably supported by her two younger assistants, known only as Hugo and Claire, who circulated amongst the discussion groups, offering encouraging words and suggesting the odd question to consider. At the end of the session some positive suggestions for affirmative language were put forward and copies of Dr Simpson's book, *Can't is a four-letter word* were on sale at a table at the back of the hall. Several copies of the book were sold, and free literature was taken. As term wore on, the title became something of a slogan amongst Princewood staff when pupils protested at the difficulty of a task, drawing a number of bemused responses.

The History Department meeting after lunch was mercifully brief as Michael Streatham was never one to waste time in banter. Bear was then able to spend time writing out class lists into his register and other necessary administrative tasks before the games meeting completed the day, at which Stuart reiterated the outcome of his earlier discussion with Fred, that rugby would remain without physical contact until the weekend, by which time the expected further rainfall should have softened the ground. After a usual pep-talk about maintaining standards on and off the field and high expectations and best wishes for all teams in all sports this term, the final meeting of the day broke up and Bear returned to his flat on the edge of town.

It had, as ever, been a 'draining straining training' day. He had forgotten which colleague had come up with that rhyming phrase, but it was certainly apt. Once he had finished his evening meal, Bear was pleased that for a change he had been organised enough to have prepared his initial series of lessons and had no further homework to complete. He settled down on his sofa and switched on the television with no intention other than to pass the time and unwind. He stumbled upon an antiques programme where a potential seller was getting a blue-and-white vase valued. The expert looked carefully at the object and his observation made Bear sit up suddenly.

'Notice the horse and rider in front of the palace. This type of craftsmanship, especially with equine themes, is not untypical of seventeenth-century Portugal and was much sought after. I would estimate that this would sell quite well.

At a conservative estimate I would say…'

I wonder, mused Bear, and the phrase 'unfinished business' came to mind. Once a very busy first week was out of the way, there was something that could not be delayed much longer.

Chapter Four
Of Ghosts and Speculation

There are few towns of comparable size to rival Princewood for its setting, historic and cultural appeal and general sense of calm. Situated about eight miles inland on the River Frame, it had been a settlement in the Saxon era and overrun by the Vikings, whose barren burial ground on a hillside overlooking the town attracted a steady stream of history buffs and school parties, and was amply supported by an alluring museum designed to emphasise the dark side of the invaders to the region with a forbidding, haunting ambience with lights dimmed. The trend towards the authentic experience of 'living history' had seen many an unsuspecting group greeted by a fearsome warrior known as Olaf the Valiant who kindly took time out from his demanding marauding duties to act as a guide around the site. Princewood's name derived from a gift made by King Henry II to one of his sons, according management of some ten square miles of dense deciduous forest land bordering on the river in 1172. The town had known prosperity in the Middle Ages through the trade in wool and served as a valuable inland port, or so the local guidebook proudly proclaimed. With a population of some fifteen thousand, Princewood in the last years of the twentieth century still drew boating enthusiasts, but almost exclusively for recreation rather than commerce. On any weekend from April to October, an assortment of craft serenely glided along the waterway, presenting a contented, comfortable, feel of a community quite happy for life to proceed at a sedate pace; taking in the often underrated beauty, of the Suffolk countryside and range of industrious wading birds at the river's edge. It was as if the twentieth century had been politely escorted out of the way to allow space for recharging of batteries and contemplation. Indeed, industry was largely confined to the manufacture of aeronautical parts at a factory a mile or so upstream, but it could have been a world away, such was the air of serenity from the gentle rhythm of river transport and unhurried strollers and cyclists following the winding riverside path.

The major attractions of the town were its two main streets, where every effort was made to accentuate the quaintness of the location, with local produce on offer in at least three shops, premises selling woollen goods and souvenir shops which advertised Princewood's historical connections and claims to fame. A section of one of the streets had been pedestrianised and produced the desired effect of locals inevitably stopping to pass the time of day with each other and being more amenable to the occasional tourist's enquiry. Apart from the hunting paradise generously provided for his offspring by a medieval monarch and the brooding burial ground, the most noteworthy historical sites were the castle that had survived the Civil War reasonably intact and the beautifully preserved eighteenth-century theatre which drew visitors from across the region and beyond. For all its touristic claims to fame, Princewood was still somewhat off the beaten track and on a warm autumn day, once schools had restarted and relative calm had returned, it was the perfect place for the retired to enjoy the views from one of the many cafés on the banks of the Frame following a leisurely amble along the riverside path. Small wonder that even some residents of long standing were in the habit of extolling the virtues of this waterside idyll.

'What a place to retire to!' Bear had once remarked to Rob McAllister while enjoying a quiet pint at The White Lion pub on a rare occasion that they were lured away from The Anchor, as they watched the sunset over the Frame.

'We're forty years too early, old boy,' Rob had responded, almost wistfully, as if their employment in the town had caused them to miss the perfect moment to appreciate Princewood to the full.

'I suppose it won't be the same if we're still here when we're sixty-five,' Bear reflected philosophically. 'If we stick at this job that long, we'll want to move somewhere quieter and slow down. Only what could be quieter than here, unless you're in a desert or somewhere?'

These same thoughts had revisited Bear on the first Saturday afternoon of term as he wandered along the riverside path, taking the air and observing the boats, noticing the regular chime of rope hitting mast that had mystified him when he first moved into town. That sound had an almost mystical allure of a siren in the twilight of an autumn evening and it had taken Bear some weeks before he identified the source. Now, several years on, it had been a hectic few days and he was glad that the first weekend, with no sports fixtures arranged, allowed him to draw breath. There had been the meeting-heavy staff training day, followed by the start of term. He had been assigned a Year 8 tutor group and had spent tutor time getting to know the group. He had not taught any of them the previous year and there were two new pupils in his group that he was eager to keep an eye on, assigning them each a buddy to look after them for the first few days. He had had a lengthy conversation with one boy's mother about relationships within the class that were rather spiky and had reassured her that after a summer's rest, new dynamics would be in play and he would keep a watchful eye out. Getting used to new classes, distributing stationery, assisting Rob with the first Under-16 training sessions, adjusting to new duties and generally refocusing on being back in a working routine after seven weeks away all took its toll. He agreed to meet up with a few of his colleagues in 'The Anchor' early that evening, but when some subsequent activities were envisaged at wilder venues, he had politely declined.

Having duly experienced a quiet weekend, Bear returned to school early on Monday morning, arriving in good time to perform any photocopying, as was his wont, or any pre-lesson tasks that might be required, allowing ample time to be waylaid by a colleague with a sudden query. Bear's Monday morning routine varied little. After completing his photocopying requirements of the day, he walked over to the humanities building, ascended the stairs to the first floor, opened up his classroom, placed the photocopied sheets on the in-tray on his desk, checked that the room was tidy and left the room, shutting the door behind him. He returned to the main building and entered the staff room to check his pigeon-hole. On this occasion there was nothing of note, except a general reminder by the deputy head that a book sale was being held in the staff room that Friday lunchtime. Bear paid little attention to the memorandum. He had no particular need for new textbooks and in any case, he was on duty for the latter part of the lunch hour that day, so he would have very little time to browse.

He looked around to see if any colleagues were lingering. Stuart Prentice was sitting in one corner having a discussion with a couple of male teachers who assisted with Games— Alan Cartwright, who coached the 3rd XV and Mike Southwood, who was responsible for the Under-14 team. Bear approached to join in the banter and was relieved, for once, that Alan had not led Stuart into another refereeing conundrum. The conversation revolved around match fitness of the first team, which had left something to be desired in their practice match against a touring team from Kent at the weekend. It was agreed that all teams should step up the fitness work that week. Bear smiled as if to indicate that he thought it was a good idea, which he did not. He would struggle keeping the Under-16B team on board over a long term as things stood without extra demands being made on their fitness. That was the trouble with whole-school initiatives. They simply did not work. It was fine Stuart planning a fitness drive for the first team, but the Under-16Bs were at the point where they knew they would soon be able to drop out of compulsory team games, and few were that enamoured of rugby football in any case. Much of Bear's motivational tactics had revolved around the joys of camaraderie in this, their last season as a separate age group, and finishing with a flourish. He did not fancy telling his charges that some bursts of interval running were to be on the agenda for the next few weeks.

Similar initiatives, often of short duration, based on a teacher's personal preferences, had emerged intermittently during Bear's relatively short career. His memory of the over-zealous former Deputy Head, Andrew Fisher, was still vivid.

Andrew had left two years before to take up a headship in Somerset, but had used his time at Princewood to set up several schemes, probably with the aim of filling his CV. One such scheme concerned his model for classroom management. Perhaps because he was a scientist and with a keen sense of the relationship between cause and effect, he encouraged, even insisted for a while, that colleagues kept a rigid seating plan for the whole academic year from which no-one deviated. Pupils were to sit in the same designated places throughout the year, facing the front, scientific practicals being one of very few prescribed exceptions. This would minimise any chatter and anchor pupils' thoughts in the aims of the lesson. This initiative had proved short-lived. The Modern Languages department, for one, was up in arms, with Claudine protesting,

''ow can zey practise zer oral work in pairs eef zey 'ave to face ze front all ze time? Eet is madness.'

Alan had wryly added that he had about seven different seating arrangements, depending on whether groups or pairs were working together. He had been known to compel classes to turn their desks around to face the back of a classroom for dictation practice, with one volunteer attempting her version on the board while the rest wrote theirs on paper with their backs to her. Andrew was dumbfounded when he entered with a visiting parent and son, not knowing how to interpret Alan's teaching methodology. The deputy head's embarrassment was compounded as none of the pupils had stood up when he entered, as was the usual courtesy, because none were aware of the newcomers thanks to Alan's habit of leaving his door ajar and in any case, his booming voice reading out the dictated extract covered the noise of those entering the classroom. Alan had somehow got away with a courteous smile and nod to the visitors and continued with the dictation, still without the class realising the deputy was in the room. Andrew had quietly left with the visitors to continue his tour. It had been a great source of amusement to Alan to ask the class if they had enjoyed Mr Fisher's visit. Of course, they thought he was having a joke. He had been able to prolong the tease for a week as the girl who wrote up the dictation (the only person who could vouch for the deputy's presence in the room) was absent with sickness for the next two lessons and could not corroborate Alan's assertion. That was enough time for the bewildered class to speculate about Andrew's stealth and he quickly acquired the nickname 'The Ghost'.

A shrill bell aroused Bear from his recollections of doomed initiatives and his limited attention to Stuart's plans to revolutionise the physical condition of the young athletes in his charge. It was time to register his class. As usual, 8H were waiting outside his classroom, ready to be admitted.

'Morning, 8H,' he greeted them cheerfully.

'Morning, sir,' most of the eighteen voices replied in unison, with a slower, mumbled response coming from a well-built but tired-looking, curly-haired twelve-year-old boy. He was a good second behind the rest of the group.

'And a good morning to you, too, Russell,' Bear said, opening the door and gesturing them all to enter and take their seats. 'Cheer up, it's only Monday morning once a week. Make the most of it!'

After taking the register and carrying out the Head's opening day message to staff to be vigilant about standards of dress by pointing out the one top button undone, he escorted the class to the school hall for the whole-school assembly, returning twenty minutes later for the first of five lessons on his schedule that day. Traditionally, the first lesson of the day can be quiet and hard work for any teacher wanting to elicit any meaningful oral contribution from a class.

Mondays were not normally too soporific, as the children were usually refreshed from the weekend and not too sleepy. Bear's first class was a group of ten Lower VI students. He had taught them just once in the previous week, enough time to set them the homework task of researching different aspects of seventeenth-century England and reporting back to the class. This task was designed as a gentle lead into the major topic of The Causes of the English Civil War. Bear had hoped that the presentations would lead to some stimulated debate on the role of parliament, but the class was not alert enough and after hearing their various contributions, applied his Plan B by inserting a video on the evolution of parliament through the ages. This invited some more lively comment in the closing minutes, at least. Something to work on, Bear thought to himself.

The second lesson was a GCSE group of fifteen students studying Major World Powers of the Twentieth Century. It had been department policy to start with Nazi Germany, 'to get it out of the way'. At this stage of term, however, Bear was leading the class through the end of the First World War with some texts on the Armistice and Treaty of Versailles and asking them whether they thought it was a fair and reasonable settlement. His chosen question, this time allowing enough time for a response, was:

'How would you feel as a German soldier on the Western Front and you thought you were doing all right and told your government had surrendered?'

Predictably, responses ranged from fury to resignation and

bewilderment. Most thought the government should be held to account. One or two questioned the poor communication that left the soldiers in the dark as to the true state of the war. Bear enjoyed this exchange of views as his class was starting to do much of his teaching for him. The discussion was just progressing purposefully as the lesson drew to a close when one boy piped up:

'But what's all this got to do with Hitler?'

'Oh, Rupert!' a collective, amused groan arose from several members of the group as if to ask whether their classmate had been listening at all.

'All will be revealed in the next exciting instalment,' was Bear's closing comment as he gestured to the class that they were free to depart.

All things considered, things were warming up nicely, and he enjoyed taking his charges through the narrative of history, maintaining just enough secrecy as if the following chapter of a gripping crime thriller was awaiting them the next time that they entered the classroom. It was a joy to him that many of his pupils embraced the spirit of discovery and assumed the hoped-for role of enthralled readers eager to find out what happened next, even if they already knew.

The third lesson, the last before morning break, usually saw pupils at their liveliest and able to participate to the full, However, on Mondays this year, Bear had a free period. He decided to use the time reading through and marking the notes that his Lower VI class had produced on the 17th century but had barely been able to settle when the challenge laid down in the antiques programme came back to him.

I must find time to get that brooch valued, he said to himself. If it's worthless, that's not so much of a problem. But if it is worth something, and the expert on the box suggested it might be, I need to make an effort to get it back to Sophie, wherever she is. He resolved to make time this week, now that the dust had settled on a new term. He returned to perusing the homework in front of him but was unable to get very far as an unmistakable gentle tap on the door indicated that his head of department would like a quick word with him.

Inwardly, Bear sighed as he knew that Michael Streatham's 'quick words' invariably extended to half a free period. So, Michael also has a free third period on a Monday this year, he noted. Last year it had been last period before lunch on a Thursday when their free periods had coincided. On more than one occasion, Bear had wanted to pop into town on a short commission but had been held up by an apparently urgent matter Michael wished to discuss. Brevity was simply not the Head of History's strong suit. He was definitely strong in clear, succinct presentation of factual information that gave his students all the ammunition they needed for detailed essays. For some reason, however, his spoken expression was anything but short and to the point. He had voiced concerns about Bear's teaching style in the past, saying he spent too much time asking questions and not enough time presenting facts. Bear had disputed this assertion, saying he directed his pupils to the sources of facts and engaged them in challenging them to picture the scenes of the period they were studying. In any case, his results backed him up that his methods were effective. Every now and again, this issue resurfaced. Bear half-expected another observation about his methodology. He was not disappointed.

'I had a chat with Mr Phelps,' Michael announced as he occupied a seat in the front row opposite Bear.

'Oh yes?' Bear replied, struggling to avoid a raised eyebrow and exasperation at the mention of that particular parent's name.

Michael clearly picked up on Bear's mood and quickly added, 'I know he's not an easy parent to get along with, but...'

'Not easy? He complains about everything. He seems to think that paying fees gives him the right to tell us how to run our business! What is it now?' Bear realised it was futile to discuss the matter they both agreed on and decided the direct approach was required.

'He felt that your approach was a little vague. He said that Amelia had struggled in Year 10 last year because she didn't understand some of the more obscure challenges you were setting.'

'She hardly struggled. She got a B in the end of year exams. With a bit more work and a little less whining she could easily get an A, as I said in her report, although using different language, you understand.'

'All I'm saying is that you might need to tone down the more hypothetical questioning and ensure that your classes, especially the GCSE classes, have sufficient clear notes on which to rely.'

'Which they do, if they care to look. Do you want me to have a word with Mr Phelps? I can give him a ring if you like.'

Bear was surprising himself by being unusually direct with his head of department. The conversation proceeded with a few examples from either side of the argument and seemed to be getting nowhere. Bear was glad that on this occasion he had no particular plans for this precious free period but made a mental note that Monday period three might be a time to make himself scarce and pay an unscheduled visit to the photocopy room to avoid these long tête-à-têtes. The quick word concluded after twenty minutes, Michael being satisfied to have discharged his responsibility in relaying parental concerns and Bear similarly relieved that the conversation had not extended until break.

A quick glance at his watch confirmed that Bear had insufficient time to begin a new project, so he inserted his pile of papers into a folder, which he slid into his in-tray, rose and left the humanities building in the direction of the staff room and his morning coffee. After pouring himself a cup, he looked across to see that there were only two early occupants of the room.

'Morning, artistes,' he greeted them warmly, finding a seat next to Christine Warmsley, Head of Art. 'Can I join the part-timers?'

'My one free of the day, I'll have you know,' she replied. 'How are things in history?'

Bear was about to say he had come to escape another session with Michael but thought better of it. He then became engaged in an absorbing conversation with Christine and her fellow art teacher, Linda Porter, on the new televised costume drama, which had begun the previous evening, and which they had all watched. Bear confessed that it was more captivating than he had anticipated and would probably continue watching. He reflected with amusement that, with the exception of Rob, this was not a conversation he would be having with most of his male colleagues.

The staff room filled up and after about ten minutes, Deputy Head David Wilkinson raised his voice.

'Ladies and gentlemen, if I could have your attention for

a second. The headmaster has asked me to say that there will be an extra staff meeting for a few minutes at two o'clock here. Unless you are on duty, it's very important that you all attend. He apologies that he can't be here now, as he's with a parent. Thank you, see you at two.'

The inevitable excited chatter dominated the last few minutes of break in the staff room. 'Pay rise, do you think?' suggested Christine hopefully.

'More likely to be a pay cut or freeze,' responded Linda.

'My money's on some scandal.' John Billington, Head of Physics, threw in his two pen'orth. 'Maybe that strange governor is leaving us suddenly.'

'Are you going to put your money where your mouth is?' challenged mathematician Roger Bulstrode. 'What do you reckon, sex or money?'

'I'll have to see what odds Fred can offer. He's probably on to it already,' John chuckled heartily.

'Inspection. It's got to be an inspection,' Alan Cartwright pronounced confidently. 'What else could it be that can't wait?'

'But we had a boarding inspection last year. They wouldn't be doing us twice in consecutive years,' John countered.

'Don't be too sure. The Independent Schools Inspection Council is a law unto itself.'

'Well, we'll soon know,' John rose without any outward expression of concern. That calm was not shared by a host of anxious faces as they filed out of the staffroom at the close of break.

* * * *

Stephen Rawlinson's known punctuality rarely failed him, and this afternoon was no exception. He stood to the right of the coffee machine at a minute to two o'clock, in front of the portrait of the school's founder, James Bromwell, who seemed to be looking down on the gathering with a wry grin. As the last stragglers shuffled into the room, the headmaster nodded to David Wilkinson to close the door and the assembled teachers fell silent.

'Ladies and gentlemen,' the Head began, 'thank you for coming at short notice. We are about to be inspected.'

Chapter Five
Foundation Books on the Road

'I'm sorry, Soph, but you're the only one who could do it.' Max Chandler was apologetic at asking his Kent and Sussex sales representative to extend her geographical orbit, but as it happened the request was well received.

'That's fine, Max. Poor Ryan! I hope he's back on his feet soon.'

'It should be a couple of weeks at least before we see him at all. After that he won't be behind a wheel for a bit. We should be able to shuffle people around to cover.'

'No problem, Max. If you can spare me from K and S?'

'Got it covered. Thanks, Soph, you're a star.'

Sophie Bingham had been called into the office of the Sales Manager of Foundation Books Limited (Education Department) on a matter of some urgency. Relieved that she was not to receive a lecture on maintaining sales targets in the region for which she was responsible, Sophie responded with shock as she learned that her colleague in the East Anglia region, Ryan Clark, had fractured his leg playing football over the weekend and would not be able to resume duties for a while. Hence the need for someone to cover some upcoming sales visits in Norfolk and Suffolk. The only staff available was the new trainee, Emily Richards, and she clearly needed an experienced hand to guide her through her first encounters with customers. Max had asked Sophie to step in and accompany Emily on a series of trips to the region. She readily agreed, reasoning that it would not hurt her career at all to be seen to be flexible. She secretly considered any range of experience, however brief, would help her to move away from the education publishing sector and apply for posts in the more lucrative fields of fiction and travel writing.

'Absolutely brill, Soph. First trip's on Friday. You haven't met Em, but you can have a good old chin wag up the A12.'

Sophie always found it amusing that Max was the only person she knew who persisted in using the shortened version of her name. He did that with all staff, without even asking. It was as if he couldn't bear addressing anyone with a name of more than syllable. Robert had automatically become Bob, Colin was reduced to Col, and the new Marketing Manager was immediately addressed as Sue before she politely but firmly said that she was to be known as Susan. It was hard, however, to be too cross with Max, as he was a genial character, a fine motivator and an accomplished salesman with a wealth of experience.

More than once in the days leading up to Friday Sophie considered the irony of an unexpected trip to Suffolk. She had remembered her pleasant couple of hours with a companionable, easy-going teacher from that county, and her hasty departure that had enabled her to catch her last bus home with a minute to spare. She reflected on her upset and exasperation at discovering that she had (probably) left the attractive bronze brooch in the café at Valença do Minho, and her mind was racing with speculation. Her flight back to the UK was booked for the following day, so returning to Valença on the off chance that the brooch was still in the café was not an option. Had Bear picked up the brooch and sought to return it to her? He seemed an honest individual, but you can never tell. If he had made efforts to contact her, she realised that neither had exchanged names of employers, nor even surnames. How dull was that? She had considered ringing up schools in the county, but quickly concluded how stupid that would have made her look. All she could do was ask for a teacher with an unusual first name. She smiled, and occasionally winced, at a potential approach:

'Excuse me, I know this might sound strange, but is there a Bear on your teaching staff?'

'I'm sorry, dear, but we don't employ wild animals here. It's against health and safety regulations, you see.'

She envisaged a host of other similar bemused, often comical responses and decided that she could not face steeling herself for a series of such painful calls. Was he taking the mickey by inventing a name, or was Bear just a nickname? He had assured her that the name was genuine with a perfectly deadpan face. If you spent your life introducing yourself as Bear, she acknowledged, you would eventually get used to it and not share the amusement of every new acquaintance hearing the name for the first time. She berated herself, the confident, extrovert saleswoman who seemed to be beaten at the first hurdle in trying to reclaim her property. But then again, maybe she had dropped the item concerned in her frantic dash back into Spain and Bear was oblivious to her loss. She decided, for now at least, that the pursuit of further enquires was futile.

Friday duly arrived with the promised return to warm September sunshine following the predicted two days of heavy rain that had affected the whole of the south-east of the country. On days like these, Sophie welcomed the opportunity to get out of London and see open countryside, not to mention the freedom of accelerating to seventy miles per hour without the constant slowing of traffic lights and jams. She had, with the help of two office staff, loaded her Nissan Micra the night before, so as to be able to set off from her Camden flat. She and Emily had been assigned two visits that day, one in Suffolk at lunchtime, followed by an after-school appearance in Essex as one of several exhibitors for a Sixth-Form college open afternoon. That worked out well, she reasoned, as she would be on her way back for the second visit, could drop Emily off and get back to London at a sensible time. There was also no rush to set off at the crack of dawn, as she was not due to pick up her younger colleague until eleven o'clock.

As arranged, she left the A12 to turn into a village just outside Colchester shortly before eleven. Emily had said she would wait on the edge of the village green, near the bus stop. She had assured Sophie that it was impossible to miss the location and was as good as her word. In any case, any doubts that Sophie might have had as to the identity of her passenger were soon dispelled as she caught sight of the slender figure looking up attentively from the green. Emily Richards was twenty-two, with straight, neatly trimmed long blonde hair, and stood out in the unmistakable uniform of Foundation Books. There was a clear air of professionalism in the combination of white blouse, lime green necktie and navy-blue skirt, with accompanying blue jacket that she was still wearing even though the day was warming up. Sophie slowed to a halt, initiated a quick exchange of pleasantries to confirm respective identities and invited her companion to come aboard.

For the forty minutes of journey before their first appointment, the two employees became better acquainted. Emily had impressed in her training and was looking forward to working around the East Anglia region, eventually under Ryan's charge when he recovered. Having determined to set her young charge at ease with a few tips, prefaced by, 'I'm sure you learned all this, but just in case…' Sophie began to fill Emily in on the two institutions they were to visit. Her explanation met with an unexpected response.

'Our first visit is to an independent school, Princewood,' Sophie began. 'Now here…'

'I know,' Emily interrupted enthusiastically. 'My aunt works in admin there. She said it might be quiet for us there today as they've got an inspection coming up next week.'

Sophie was taken aback. Her young colleague was well informed.

'I'd forgotten you were local. Just didn't know you were that local. So, you know Princewood?'

'Not really. My aunt works there, as I say, and her son Andy, my cousin, is in Year 10, just starting his GCSEs.'

'And how did you know about this inspection?'

'The whole office staff know. Letters have been drawn up to send to parents for a questionnaire of customer satisfaction or something. She's been doing a bit of overtime. The thing is, she reckons there won't be much interest in buying new books as all the teachers will be interested in is keeping their records up to date and their classrooms tidy. They won't have time for the likes of us.'

'Not necessarily,' Sophie quickly responded. 'It can work both ways. They may decide they need to be seen to be moving with the times and want to freshen up their personal libraries to be seen to be progressive and get them some brownie points with the inspectors, or at least with the head teacher. We could yet have a busy old lunch hour.'

Shortly afterwards the Foundation Books duo reached their destination. Princewood School comprised a combination of nineteenth- and twentieth-century buildings and its prominent main building, known as Bromwell House, was an imposing presence at the end of a lengthy entrance drive. It was one of the older buildings on site and contained the offices of the head and his deputies, admin offices and the staff room. The wooden décor inside gave off an impression of permanence, reflecting the Tudor origins of the site. The first school in the town had been set up under the brief reign of Edward VI, but the boys' grammar school had been an establishment for protestant dissenters since the late eighteenth century. Tradition has a tendency to be deep-rooted and though the school had been completely co-educational for over a quarter of a century, teachers were still asked by older residents how they found the 'lads' at the school.

Once Sophie had pulled into the school car park, there was barely time to admire the architectural features or the expansive grounds before reporting to the school office, where a receptionist greeted them and summoned a member of office staff to direct the visitors to the staff room. Emily briefly poked her nose into her aunt's office to say hello, eager not to hold Sophie up. Surveying the room's layout, Sophie suggested a corner at which they could set up their stall. This was agreed, and as the car park was a few minutes' walk from the staffroom, the Foundation Books pair had to make four trips to extract all the wares required. By the time Sophie had erected the impressive pop-up stand with the company logo and prominent picture of an enthusiastic teacher spouting from a publication to an equally keen, smiling class, time had moved on to half-past twelve. Just time for a quick bite of packed lunch before expecting any early customers at the pre-arranged starting time of a quarter to one. Then, the theory was that she and Emily should prepare themselves for a frantic hour and a half. In practice some visits were extremely quiet and soul-destroying. Sophie had experienced both scenarios and had few clues as to which way this one would turn out.

In fact, her earlier hunch that there might be heightened interest seemed justified, much to her gratification, not just from the thrill of completing book sales and taking orders but for her credibility in correctly alerting her young colleague. There had been several teachers who, responding to David Wilkinson's memo or their own interest in expanding their resources, engaged their visitors in conversation at different points in the lunch hour and several orders were secured and a number of textbooks purchased on the spot, mainly relating to changes in GCSE specifications. By a quarter to two most staff were aware of Foundation Books' distinct presence on site.

It was at this time that Bear was lingering over lunch, still troubled at how to rearrange his classroom display in readiness for the trials of the following week. He was eager to make the history trip the previous spring to Roundham Castle more central, as its Civil War connections tied in very well with the current syllabus and had proved valuable in recruiting students to study history further. The quality of photos taken that day was variable, however, and he was not sure if uprooting the material so carefully assembled would be worth the trouble. If he did make such radical alterations, he would have to complete them after school as Friday was a very full day for him that year. In addition to a full day of lessons, he was due out on duty at five to two, which involved patrolling the areas most populated with children for twenty minutes before afternoon classes began. His participation in conversation in the dining hall was limited, a few remarks exchanged with Rob about the visit of the Under-16 teams the following day to Frameborough, and some comments on the week ahead. He had caught snatches of John Billington's conversation with Roger Bulstrode, during which the former had asked the latter if he had met the air hostesses. Roger had responded with the words 'attractive' and 'well turned-out', Bear thought, but he could not see any reason to turn his thoughts to air travel to exotic destinations.

He rose from lunch a few minutes before his duty period was due to begin. Normally, on a fine day, Bear was happy to venture outside early, and was about to do so when for no explicable reason, he decided he would head to the staff room for a few minutes' quiet contemplation before taking over from the colleague about to come off duty.

Turning into the staff room, he noticed the Foundation Books stand at the far corner, and immediately remembered that this company were selling their wares at lunchtime. Bear smiled as he caught sight of a young blonde woman whose attire, he affirmed, perfectly fitted John's earlier description. There was another visiting salesperson engaged in light-hearted chatter with Christine Warmsley, completing an order for art books, but this person was obscured from his view by Christine and another teacher. Bear decided five minutes glancing at what Foundation Books had to offer would break up the monotony of the day and approached the table cheerily.

It was at that moment that the art teacher took her leave gratefully and vacated space in front of the senior visiting salesperson.

'I'll be with you in a moment,' said Sophie, without looking up as she completed filling in a form.

'That's quite all right,' replied Bear, grinning. 'After all, I think you've been the one kept waiting for a few weeks now.'

At this mysterious remark Sophie looked up, her jaw dropped, and she was momentarily speechless for one of the few occasions in her sales career.

Chapter Six
An Improbable Reunion

'Your round, Bear, I do believe.'

As Rob McAllister's prompt had met with no response, amused glances were exchanged around the table at The Anchor Inn that Friday evening in September. A smaller gathering than before term started, the six teachers at Princewood School were enjoying a pre-inspection week drink and the conversation had been hearty, occasionally laced with anxiety. Rob and Stuart were regulars at the Anchor; Rachel made an occasional appearance when not pursuing what seemed a long-distance relationship with her boyfriend; close neighbours Samantha Dixon, in charge of girls' PE and Alan Cartwright lived close to the pub and joined in intermittently if family commitments allowed; Bear completed the sextet, but had become noticeably quieter as the hour had worn on.

'There are ways of waking someone from a catatonic trance,' suggested Rachel.

'Don't be cruel. He's obviously got a lot on his mind,' interjected Samantha.

'Haven't we all?' reflected Alan.

It was only when Rachel decided to refrain from whatever shock tactics that had crossed her mind and resorted to a slow wave of the hand across Bear's face that her historian colleague abruptly awoke from his reverie.

'I'm sorry. I was miles away. What was that?' he asked, flustered.

'About fifty miles away, headquarters of a certain education publishers, I would estimate,' Rob suggested with a knowing smile.

'I'll get the next round,' offered Stuart. 'Same again?'

As Stuart headed to the bar for refills, Rob turned to Bear and added, 'I do believe our Bear is well and truly smitten this time.'

'Either that, or he's been in hibernation,' quipped Alan.

'It's not like that,' Bear protested. 'It's just such an amazing coincidence. I am struggling to make sense of things.'

'So you said,' said Rob.

Bear had indeed explained his reason for an extraordinary conversation with a young lady he now knew to be called Sophie Bingham that lunchtime. Or, more accurately, he had been pressed into explaining how they knew each other, first by Rob and Stuart when they arrived, then shortly afterwards in shorter versions to Rachel, then Alan and Samantha, when they appeared. There is nothing more irritating than having to reveal something slightly embarrassing repeatedly, Bear reflected, knowing that unless an explanation is forthcoming, the rumour mill will only expand to his cost. If only he could post a notice on the staff room board to say: Sophie Bingham is someone I met on holiday whose brooch happened to be left in my hands by mistake. End of story. No, that would not work. There was no way of explaining the encounter without a precise, painstaking re-telling of the incident in Portugal.

Some of Bear's colleagues had witnessed the reunion earlier that day. After Sophie had controlled her amazement at seeing her former café companion, she had managed to utter some coherent words.

'Of all the schools in Suffolk to visit. I had no idea you worked here!'

'And I had no idea which company you worked for,' Bear had responded. 'I've been meaning to contact you... or at least try to. I've got something of yours.'

'My brooch? That's amazing! It was really stupid of me to leave it behind. I can be so absent-minded at times.'

'No, no. It was me who was stupid. It was lying on the table for twenty minutes and I got so lost in my book. By the time I realised it was too late and you were over the border, at least I assumed you were... unless the bus was late, that is...'

'No, it wasn't late,' Sophie confirmed to Bear's relief, more because he had been right in judging he had insufficient time to pursue her than through concern that she could have been stranded on the wrong side of the border for a night.

'Have you got it with you?' she asked.

'Got what? Oh, the brooch...' Bear had started to think how he could return the item to its owner. 'It's at home. I'm afraid I've got to go on duty now. How long are you here for?'

Sophie had confirmed that she and Emily were due to pack up at a quarter past two to head to their second appointment of the afternoon and were not due in the county again for a few weeks. She added that she was not normally in the region and explained about Ryan's incapacity. Bear confessed, no offence meant, that he had forgotten all about Foundation Books' scheduled visit but for some reason chose to drop in on the staff room for five minutes.

'Perhaps that's just fate we met again?' wondered Sophie.

'Something like that, possibly.'

A few teachers were within earshot of this exchange,

keeping a discreet but amused distance, pretending to be involved in other business. Sophie had hurriedly presented Bear with her business card, and on reflection, added her mobile number on the back, aware that an obviously personal conversation during office hours might not go down so well, even with a boss as genial and accommodating as Max Chandler. Bear had just enough time to write down his number before apologising profusely that he had to be outside on duty. It wouldn't do to be seen to be late for duty, especially just prior to an inspection.

That had been the extent of their conversation, much to the bewilderment of those present in the staff room. Hence the continuation of the theme of Bear's new acquaintance over a few pints that evening. Rob had tried to probe deeper, playfully suggesting Bear could use the unplanned temporary possession of Sophie's property to maximum advantage, to be returned at a time when she was obliged to have time for him. Although Bear had thought about the return of the brooch repeatedly over the past few weeks, that was one course of action that had not occurred to him. As the evening wore on and the other members of the group drifted away, Stuart engaged Bear and Rob in rugby-related chat and wished his colleagues well as he did not expect to see them before the fixtures with Frameborough College the following day, as they were playing at different venues; the first team were entertaining Frameborough's finest on Fred's immaculately prepared early-season turf, while the Under-16 teams were making the half-hour coach trip north for their matches.

* * * *

Frameborough College was a smaller independent school than Princewood. There were rumours that it was struggling for numbers with parents voting with their feet and deciding to keep their offspring within the state sector. On the sports field they were competitive, but Princewood would normally expect to win most contests, although on occasion a combination of raw determination from Frameborough and over-confidence from their opponents had led to surprise results in the past. Stuart had stressed the importance of vigilance to all sides to prevent any unnecessary embarrassment. This was one of the schools that just about managed to field two teams per age group, so Bear was inwardly confident his charges would triumph. His manufactured team talk, with a few key buzz words such as 'commitment', 'discipline', 'look after the ball' carefully emphasised, followed by regular remonstration from the touchline, proved to be the extent of Bear's responsibilities for the afternoon. His Under-16B team scored early on, and although the home side had its moments they were eventually worn down and Bear's team emerged the victors by some thirty points.

The under-16A fixture was a much closer affair. As was customary, this match kicked off later than the B fixture, enabling the players who had just finished their contest to witness the closing stages of the A match and cheer on their fellows. Bear having caught sight of an anxious Rob McAllister on the touchline, enquired as to the score, to be told that Princewood held a narrow lead. Rob muttered something about 'stupid decisions' by his team. When questioned by Bear as to whether this assessment applied to the referee, Rob quickly answered,

'Let's not go there.'

Fine, thought Bear, I get the message.

After Princewood weathered a determined surge by the home team to secure victory with a late try and the two teachers exchanged notes in the inevitable post-mortem on the coach trip home, Bear ventured to suggest that the outcome could not have been better. Rob, dissatisfied with his team's showing, was not so sure.

'On another day, against better opposition, we would have lost. Too much complacency. They believe what everyone has been saying about them. Too much praise. It's gone to their heads.'

'No problem,' countered Bear with the calmness of a private detective declaring the dénouement of a mystery lesser mortals could not fathom. 'You just need to use our result as motivation. Say how impressed Mr Hoskins was with the B team and that he thinks several should be pushing for places in the A team next week.'

'Were you that impressed?'

'No. But does it matter? A bit of psychology will work much better than any of Stuart's fitness drives.'

'Don't tell me you've been reading it as well!' Rob gave his colleague a quizzical look.

'Been reading what?' asked Bear, puzzled.

With that Rob reached into his jacket pocket and produced a notebook-sized paperback publication, still in excellent condition as he had only bought it the previous day: *Doing It My Way—Motivational Strategies for Teachers*, published by Foundation Books Ltd.

* * * *

On return to Princewood, Rob had surprisingly declined Bear's suggestion of joining their fellow rugby coaches for a post-match pint in The Anchor, a regular feature of the autumn term for those having overseen home fixtures, and those returning from away ones if not too distant, as was the case with that Saturday. Bear had raised an eyebrow and observed that Rob must have urgent business to attend to, to which his friend replied with a grin and a thumbs-up. There was no need for Bear to pursue matters further, as he knew that romantic matters arising from the holiday were clearly in progress. Bear entered the pub at half-past six to note that five male colleagues were occupying a table near to where he had spent the previous evening.

'How did you get on today, Bear?' asked Chris Blanchard, Director of Studies, Chemistry teacher and in charge of the second fifteen. 'Don't tell be you've been "framed"!' he added dramatically, employing the colourful expression translated as 'beaten by Frameborough', known only to Princewood games staff.

'No, no "framings" to report, I'm pleased to say.' Bear filled the assembled group in on events away from home, before being informed in turn that the first team had had to work hard for a laboured victory (running out of steam in the last quarter, explained Stuart, indicating his preference of remedy in training the following week) and the only two sides 'framed' were the Under-15 teams.

'Looks like you're first to wear the tie, Phil,' Alan Cartwright turned to Phil Parsons, in charge of the Under-15A team whose result was the worst of the afternoon with a twenty-point defeat. The tradition among the games staff was that the teacher whose team experienced the worst outcome the previous Saturday was obliged to wear a particularly garish, floral, crimson tie on the following Saturday. The tie had been purchased on a whim by a former colleague during a visit to Singapore some years ago and it certainly stood out in a crowd. The buyer had been only too happy to bequeath the tie to the P.E. department on his departure to pastures new. It was certainly a source of amusement among the merry band of coaches, although its motivational value to a team eager not to see their coach donning the unwanted garment on successive weeks was dubious.

'I suspect I may be getting well acquainted with our crimson friend over the coming weeks,' Phil commented ruefully. He knew that his team was seen as particularly weak that year and contemplated a long season ahead.

A jovial half-hour ensued, punctuated by the inevitable refereeing issue raised by Alan, before the group dispersed. The rest of the weekend was relatively quiet for Bear. A first full week had taken its toll and he had not ventured out any further that evening. The Sunday morning service at Grove Street Baptist Church contained a thoughtful sermon by the Rev Michael Standish on 'letting your light shine before all men', based on a passage in the Sermon on the Mount. Bear had the uncomfortable feeling that he was being encouraged to hold nothing back and let the world inspect every corner of his life. Was this what I wanted to hear just before inspection week? He was collared at the end of the service by Cynthia, Michael's wife, and asked if he was coming to an open planning meeting for the Christmas services on Thursday evening. Bear's initial protestation that they had not got through the Harvest Festival service yet was countered by Cynthia cheerfully extolled the virtues of planning ahead; he felt compelled to add a supplementary explanation, excusing himself on the grounds of a busy inspection week ahead. After that excuse had been graciously accepted with a 'We'll miss your input. Well, if you change your mind', Bear left with a degree of guilt, since he knew that the inspection would have finished by Thursday afternoon.

Bear felt further unease as the evening wore on. As he attended to his marking and preparation for the week from four o'clock onwards, he found concentrating elusive. Not just in view of the week ahead, but because he knew he needed to contact Sophie. He had to make some arrangement to return the brooch that had been his unwanted property for some weeks now. He was uncertain as to when the transfer could be made with a busy schedule, including weekends, ahead. Finally, realising he could put it off no longer, he dialled Sophie's number. He was about to hang up after several rings when she picked up.

'Hello?'

'Sophie? It's Bear, Bear Hoskins from Princewood School,' he announced, instantly berating himself for sounding so formal, as if he was organising delegates for a history conference and checking on their likely attendance.

'Bear. How are you?' she replied, warmly. 'Is it okay to call you Bear?'

'Of course. It's my name. My real name, in case you have doubts.'

'No doubts at all,' she lied. 'I'm glad you rang. Sorry we didn't have time to talk much on Friday.'

'No, I'm sorry I had to dash off. I hope you had a successful day.' We're becoming a double act in competing to be the leading apologiser, he concluded to himself with a wry smile.

'Very successful. You teachers were keen on placing orders. I think your inspection has focused some minds.'

'Ah, the inspection. What a cheery subject! Moving swiftly on,' Bear answered jovially, taking advantage of the obvious opportunity to move away from small talk and cut to the chase. 'When can I get your brooch back to you?'

He explained that this term it was difficult getting away at weekends as Saturdays were mainly tied up with rugby fixtures but suggested a date in early October when his B team were idle. This proved unworkable, as Sophie was attending a wedding that day. As she was not due in Suffolk in the near future, Bear suggested meeting in London at the earliest convenience. He offered to send the brooch in the post but said he would hesitate to do so on account of the value of the item. He felt curiously glad when she readily agreed that it was wise to avoid the postal route.

'In any case, I think I ought to thank you in person for looking after the brooch,' she added.

What did she mean by that, Bear wondered? He did not dwell on that thought but seized the initiative.

'How does this sound? My sister lives in Surrey and she will be away on holiday with her family at half-term all week. I've agreed to occupy their house and do some cat-sitting. How about meeting up on the Saturday if you're free?'

Sophie confirmed that she was and looked forward to meeting Bear then, and they agreed to decide on a time and place nearer the date. After a few moments' light-hearted chat about the feline to be in Bear's charge, he excused himself by saying he had further pre-inspection prep to finish. There were additional reciprocal apologies that it would be a few more weeks before Sophie was reunited with her property, and the conversation ended.

Sliding open his desk's top drawer, Bear picked up the brooch and gazed at it with admiration. It was certainly a fine piece of craftsmanship, even his untrained eye had to acknowledge. Whilst relieved to have secured some plan for its return, he still felt uneasy. Sophie had been relaxed about the delay, displaying neither the anxiety nor the urgency that one would expect from someone separated from a valuable ornament. Was she really assuming that it was not worth much? Bear hated the thought of handing the brooch back to Sophie without either of them knowing its value. The words of the antiques expert on television were still fresh in his memory. He resolved to get to the bottom of the issue. He had a free date between now and the planned rendezvous with Sophie. Once the inspection was out of the way, he would make the most of it.

Chapter Seven
Inspectors Calling

If it could be levelled at Princewood School that any of their procedures lacked rigour, the conduct of the whole-school Monday morning assembly was not one of them. The routine of gathering six hundred students, along with forty staff, into the school hall and dispersing them efficiently afterwards, was well established. This was one feature of school life that needed no special rehearsal prior to the much-awaited inspection week. On this Monday in September, their numbers were increased by one visitor, namely the lead inspector, Dr Anthony Hopkinson. He had arrived at the school early, ahead of the rest of the team, with the intention of spending time in interviews with the Head and his deputies in the morning before meeting up with his inspector colleagues in the afternoon.

Shortly after a quarter to nine, as was the established practice, a youthful figure emerged from the front of the auditorium and made her way to the centre aisle. Having received a signal from the duty staff member that the headmaster and his deputies were ready to enter the hall, Head Girl Sarah Shawcross briskly walked to the designated position as the assembled student body rose to their feet. It was the duty of one of the six senior prefects to call the assembled throng to order on a Monday morning and was one of the most visible, albeit brief, expressions of praefectorial privilege. She paused purposefully and called out, 'Quiet, please!' and retired to the side of the hall, at which any residual murmured conversation subsided. On cue, Stephen Rawlinson deliberately strode down the aisle. He cut an imposing figure. Silver-haired, tall and slim, in his late fifties and with fifteen years' experience as a headteacher behind him, he was dressed in a dark grey suit with a navy-blue tie carrying insignia from his Cambridge boating days. Over his clothes he was wearing an academic gown, as were Angela Banks, Senior Deputy in charge of pastoral affairs, and David Wilkinson, who followed the Head and brought up the rear of the stage party. Between Stephen and Angela walked Dr Hopkinson as the invited guest for the morning, not that the invitation had been issued by anyone at Princewood.

Once the party of four had carefully climbed the half-dozen steps to the stage and reached their positions in front of their designated seats, Sarah Shawcross again announced in her shrill voice, 'Let us begin our assembly by singing hymn number one hundred and forty-three.'

There was a rustling of scarlet hymn books as the indicated page was located; then, to the right of the congregation at the front, leading sixth-form pianist Arthur Chang played the opening bars of 'He who would valiant be' under the watchful gaze of Director of Music, Mark Spedding, who, with a purposeful flourish, gestured to the gathering that they needed to engage their voices and participate. The singing that morning was robust and reasonably tuneful, which was not always the case. No surprises today, teachers commented at the end of the assembly with cursory comments exchanged on their way to classes. Get the star musician to perform at the beginning of inspection week in front of the lead inspector and select a booming hymn that we all know.

Fred would have put his shirt on both decisions, others commented.

There was certainly a distinctly upbeat tone set by the assembly. The scripture subsequently read out by another prefect was 'I can do anything through Christ who strengthens me' from Paul's first letter to the Corinthians and was reinforced by succinct but forceful prayers by Chaplain Martin Bickersdike, delivered in his rich Lancashire accent that twenty years of living in Suffolk had failed to eradicate. The phrase 'naw boondries to what we can achieve' was his positive take on the Apostle Paul's statement. Stephen Rawlinson was not slow in following on the theme to the extent that many staff wondered if the whole presentation was elaborately rehearsed by chaplain and Head beforehand. Yes, observed Stephen Rawlinson, there are no boundaries to what we can achieve if we put our minds to it, after the students were seated and he began his weekly notices and mini-homily, or thought for the week. He announced the encouraging sports results over the weekend with the positive balance of outcomes both in the rugby fixtures against Frameborough and in the girls' hockey matches against St. Catherine's, a smaller girls' private school, who, like Frameborough, were opponents that Princewood were expected to beat.

'Frameborough… Saint Caths… couldn't have chosen better opponents if we tried,' John Billington was to remark, unable to suppress a grin, as he left the hall at the end, 'especially prior to inspection.'

'You're surely not suggesting collusion, are you, Billers?' responded Roger Bulstrode, raising an eyebrow in mock severity, at which the Head of Physics chuckled to himself.

Stephen Rawlinson read out a couple of announcements concerning orchestra practice times and auditions for the school play which would commence soon, either of which could have been dealt with through other channels but added an extra vibrancy to proceedings. He then introduced Dr Hopkinson, explaining the latter's purpose in being present that week, as he was sure they all knew, as parents had been informed of the coming inspection. His guest was invited to say a few words, which were duly delivered with a restrained smile, Dr Hopkinson saying that he expected business as usual, not to be alarmed if a visitor came into their classroom, and he was sure that that he and his team would see many signs of the excellent standards for which Princewood was justly renowned. He would enjoy meeting many of them and he was very much looking forward to the week. With that, Stephen Rawlinson drew proceedings to a close and the assembly broke up in a reasonably orderly fashion.

A relatively uneventful beginning to the teaching week did little to alleviate the growing anxiety that Bear was experiencing. Two fairly subdued classes preceded his free third period, during which he was not honoured with a little chat with Michael Streatham. The Head of History had, no doubt, other things to attend to before the serious business of being inspected began. Bear's unease was not just the urgency to get to the end of Thursday and celebrate, hopefully with good cause, the departure of a team from ISIC for another six years. He was conscious of other matters he needed to pursue, and unwanted property he wished to return as soon as possible. The lot of the schoolmaster or schoolmistress, especially in an independent school where extra-curricular contribution was expected on several fronts, was such that it meant that opportunities to exit the educational bubble were few and far between. With the exception of sports fixtures, it was rare for Bear or his colleagues to venture out of the county in term time, especially during the busy autumn term. In a rare quiet moment that day, he reflected that his adventures in Portugal seemed a world away.

At breaktime the staff had been asked to assemble for a few words from Dr Hopkinson. As a result, the movement to and from the coffee jugs was brisker and less ponderous than usual. Conversation inevitably turned to the week ahead.

'I hope my Year 10s are a bit livelier if they get inspected than they were just now,' remarked biologist Jill Carpenter, wearily seating herself in one of the more comfortable armchairs in the corner of the staffroom, 'couldn't get anything out of them, not that made any sense.'

'Are you sure you didn't dazzle them with long words like "photosynthesis", my dear?' asked John Billington mischievously. 'After all, the likes of Will Durham can't cope with anything over two syllables until at least noon.'

'He's just the sort of person to come up with some off the wall question out of nowhere. He can be quiet all lesson, then suddenly, he'll ask something ridiculous like... I don't know, I might plan a surprise test for Wednesday. That will at least keep them quiet, in case the inspector calls.'

'Didn't know you were into J B Priestley, Jill. *An Inspector Calls?*' mused Rob McAllister. 'Maybe we should study the play in Year 11 this week, just for a laugh.'

'Don't jest,' Peter Walton, Bear's colleague in the history department cut in, joining a group of half a dozen sitting in that corner. 'I know of one over-zealous English teacher who did just that. Abandoned the syllabus for that week and started on just that play. He even based his homework on the qualities of an inspector, with some highly provocative remarks about the requirements of the job being to invade people's privacy, to be sly and ruthless in spotting the tiniest speck of malpractice.'

'No-one round here, was it?' asked Jill, concerned.

'I couldn't possibly say,' responded Peter mysteriously, 'save to say that that he was given to such mood swings and was eventually given the old heave-ho.'

Jill knew better than to respond further to Peter's colourful selection of phrases, for which he was renowned to the extent of being a personal trademark, on a par with his collection of striking bow ties. Today he was sporting a scarlet number with white dots, contrasting with the bright yellow shirt he had elected to wear. He can get away with anything, she reflected and concluded that his dress sense complemented perfectly his exuberant style of teaching, as Bear had often been able to confirm, operating as he did in the nearest classroom and able to hear the most passionate exclamations from his colleague.

Her train of thoughts was interrupted, and the conversation stilled, by Stephen Rawlinson entering the room, accompanied by Anthony Hopkinson. As the staffroom fell silent, the headmaster introduced their visitor and invited him to address the gathering. The lead inspector duly smiled and explained his plans for the week to a sea of curious faces. Some staff were anxious, some had heard it all before, others were genuinely interested in the speech that an inspector would deliver. In fact, Dr Hopkinson kept it short, saying he and his inspection team would drift in at the beginning of a lesson. If a sheet could be left on a vacant back table with the lesson plan for the lesson to be inspected, there should be no need for interruptions or for the teacher's flow to be disturbed. He and his team promised to be discreet.

'It will be as if we are ghosting in and out,' the inspector concluded with a smile.

At this remark John Billington cupped a firm palm to his face as several grins were exchanged around that table, and Jill Carpenter placed an admonishing hand on his elbow to reinforce the inappropriateness of mirth. Any sniggering engendered by the recollections of the previous deputy head was thankfully drowned out by the Head's expression of thanks to his visitor and wishing everyone a successful week.

'All I can say is I'm glad the inspection is now and not nearer to Hallowe'en,' John announced when conversation levels returned to a volume at which he could speak freely. 'I think I would have had nightmares about a certain former colleague's deathly approach.'

'I blame Mac myself. Suggesting studying *An Inspector Calls*! That's probably put a curse on the week!' concluded Peter Walton.

'And who brought up this weird English teacher with the inspector obsession in the first place?' Rob retorted, enjoying the verbal joust, before adding, 'I suppose inspection week can do strange things to people. It can cause even the most rational to act in odd ways.'

Further speculation about any gloomy foreboding was cut short by the two-minute warning bell for the end of break and the majority of teachers who were not fortunate to have a free period rose to return to their respective classrooms.

* * * *

The next three days passed surprisingly quickly, as is often the case when a group of people's minds are fully occupied. The remainder of the inspection team arrived late on Monday and were introduced to the staff at Tuesday breaktime, after which they proceeded to head in different directions to inspect lessons, examine documentation and engage in a series of interviews with staff as to how the school was run. Bear was initially anxious as Peter Walton proved particularly flamboyant in his delivery, even for him, in pronouncing on the Gunpowder Plot and how close this country came to disaster. He challenged a Year 9 class with the question of how they would deal with a terrorist such as Guy Fawkes. Bear was teaching his Upper Sixth group of eight pupils, leading a discussion on the abolition of slavery, when a thunderous bellow of 'Terrorist!' resounded from the adjacent classroom. It transpired that this was one of the classes that had been inspected. Peter, sporting a silver bow tie with orange zig-zag stripes, cheerfully reported that the inspector seemed to have been impressed with his captivating tour de force. Bear wondered if he could match such heights of passion.

In fact, he was pleasantly surprised. He was inspected twice. Mrs Da Souza, an amiable woman in her late fifties, took her allotted place at the back of his classroom and listened to his conduct of a Year 7 class, in which Bear was able to conduct a debate on the events of 1789 and the Storming of the Bastille, asking how the eleven-year-olds would have felt under the hardship of the Ancien Régime. An enthusiastic response was elicited. The other lesson chosen for inspection, the following day, was another Year 11 class, following on from the previous reflection on the end of the First World War and focused on the post-war economic crisis in Germany. Was it inevitable that the Versailles settlement was harsh on Germany or could another solution have been found? he asked. After a few opinions had been expressed, he pressed the empathy button, conscious to avoid using the all-too familiar wording. So, he asked, what would have been uppermost in your mind if you had been an ordinary citizen in the aftermath of defeat in this international conflict? Bear had every reason to feel that his delivery, engagement with the pupils and subject knowledge had been positively acknowledged by Mrs Da Souza.

On the Wednesday afternoon, Bear had been asked by the deputy head to join a group of colleagues to be quizzed on communication and administrative procedures. Half a dozen selected teachers, none of them Heads of Department, had been chosen, as those on the receiving end of requests, directives and various other missives and asked if they were being informed effectively. Bear noticed that the newest member of staff, Karen Dempsey, who had joined the English department at the start of term, was included, to give a newcomer's perspective, so that the inspector could tell whether she had been suitably briefed on school procedures. To David Wilkinson's credit, he had anticipated such a meeting taking place and the answers were well rehearsed. The inspector chairing this meeting seemed satisfied with the responses to the various hypothetical scenarios he posed and was happy to dismiss the group after about twenty-five minutes. As Thursday wore on, Bear received no further inspector's visits. Mrs Da Souza seemed satisfied with what she had seen from the two lessons she had witnessed and when Thursday lunchtime came around, he was breathing a sigh of relief.

'Nearly there, Bear,' Rob smiled at Bear as he placed his tray next to his friend having been served his lunch.

'That should be it as far as the inspecting business goes,' Bear responded with satisfaction. 'Unless they want to inspect our rugby practice this afternoon? Stranger things have happened, I suppose.'

'I doubt it. The games inspector has been out regularly all three days. He's thoroughly quizzed Stu and Samantha, and I suspect he will want to get on with preparing his notes. But just in case, I have something planned for this afternoon. A slight change of schedule...'

'Oh yes?' Bear asked, and listened to his fellow-coach's plan, nodding supportively but not without a nagging misgiving.

* * * *

'Unopposed?' At least three voices from the Under-16 Rugby squad responded with incredulity. 'But it's Thursday!' another voice added his protestation.

'It's a form of unopposed, call it semi-opposed,' explained Rob McAllister. 'The A team will run through their moves and the Bs will provide no opposition, no contact, no tackling. They will just track the A team's attack and when they touch an attacker, we will assume there is a breakdown in play and the A team will recycle the ball and continue their attack. Then the Bs will do the same to the As. Once we've run through everything, we'll put it into practice with a game at the end.' His explanation was met with a sea of puzzled faces, some grinning, some expressing suspicion, others just keen to get on with things. Bear, whose job was to marshal his B team as defenders, encouraged his troops to look lively and not stand around discussing things but was not entirely convinced that his colleague had chosen the best strategy for the afternoon's practice. His unease increased as he noticed the games inspector making his way to the field, clipboard in hand.

Bear knew that Rob had a tendency to act on impulse and change his plans for no apparent reason. Rob's impulsiveness had got him into difficulty in romantic liaisons in the past. Bear could never understand why his colleague did not simply back his judgement instead of trying to extract something extra from a situation. As the players assumed their positions for the unopposed session, Bear had the distinct feeling that the exercise would not yield the coach's desired result. He was swiftly to be proved right. 'Unopposed' was a part of rugby training sessions usually reserved for a short, gentle run-out on Friday afternoons before the match on a Saturday. It was standard practice that school teams would run through their repertoire with no opposition to disturb them and not overdo the physical exertion, saving their energy for the following day. Friday was meant for brief tweaking of tactics, allowing for any changes of plan occasioned, say, by the expected absence of a player and need for his replacement to adjust.

Thursday's training was always a more whole-hearted affair, often determining any selection changes for the weekend. However, the news that the less intense activity had been brought forward a day had puzzled many of the Under-16 group. To have to rein in their aggression had created a listlessness, bordering on apathy among many of the players and it was not lost on them that the inspector was keeping a close eye on proceedings.

It was clear to Bear what Rob's intentions were, however flawed they appeared. Rob was convinced that a display of well-rehearsed moves would show off his team's military precision and impress any watching inspector. Unfortunately, he greatly underestimated his charges' reluctance to adapt to the change in schedule. Within a few seconds of the A team receiving the ball from a kick-off, the ball was dropped. In the contrived form of the game in operation, Rob awarded a free-kick to the A team to enable them to practise a set move.

'It should be our scrum, sir!' protested one of the B team, 'they knocked it on.'

'Quiet, Basham, play to the whistle!' Bear admonished, hoping Rob did not have to resort to more creative refereeing.

His hopes were dashed as a litany of handling errors followed; passes were dropped or overthrown, moves went wrong through players bumping into one another and the general standard of play was fast becoming embarrassing. The B team asked if they could be given the opportunity to run through their moves and in a brief pause in play as Rob theatrically reminded his three-quarter line of the correct alignment, audible enough for the inspector to understand, another wisecrack emanated from the ranks of the understudy team.

'Excuse me, sir, should we be practising all our moves in front of a visitor? I mean, he could be a spy for Brandford for all we know.' Brandford College were Princewood's opponents that coming Saturday.

'No, you wally!' cut in another voice. 'He's an inspector!'

'What if he's inspecting Brandford tomorrow? He could pass all our secrets on,' a third chipped in.

Bear had had about enough of the shambles and was about

to intervene when fortunately, Rob agreed to hand the baton over to the B team to show off their moves.

Bear seized the moment. 'It had better be better than the As. One unforced error and the whole team runs to the posts and back.... And that rule continues throughout the real game that follows.'

'That's right,' Rob quickly agreed as if the decision was all part of the pre-session planning.

With that the standard improved markedly; there were a few punishment-runs to the posts imposed but as the unopposed session finally was replaced by a competitive game, a reasonable level of play emerged and after thirty minutes of action the session drew to a close, the inspector having moved on half-way through.

'He missed the best bit,' Rob reflected ruefully to Bear at the end. 'What I don't quite understand is why you...' Bear began.

'Just don't,' Rob cut in. 'Shall we just draw a line under today?' He paused, then added, 'Maybe today has been helpful. We can tell them tomorrow what would happen if they made that number of errors against Brandford.'

'Great psychology, Mac. Let me guess, covered in chapter three of *Doing It My Way*? Another classic motivational strategy?'

Rob's sheepish grin told Bear all he needed to know about his colleague's reading habits during the fraught inspection week.

A brief visit to the town centre for a couple of items proved to lighten Bear's mood at the end of the day. Knowing that the inspection had concluded that afternoon put his mind at rest, but he was still buzzing from the experience of the near-disastrous training session and the pleasant surroundings of the market town in the warm autumn sunshine only partially cleared his mind of the events of the week. He needed to get away from thinking of school matters. The thought of spending an evening sitting at home and stewing over school business did not appeal, still less, meeting colleagues for a post-inspection drink at The Anchor where there would inevitably be one dominant, suffocating topic of conversation. Any opportunity to spend time that evening outside the Princewood School bubble would be immensely appealing, not to say therapeutic. What happened next was unexpected but whose significance would not become clear for several weeks.

At that moment he turned a corner on his way back to school when he almost literally bumped into Cynthia Standish, who smiled and greeted him warmly. He did not allow the pastor's wife to broach any topic of church affairs but aimed a pre-emptive strike that he had not anticipated,

'Can't stop just now, Cynthia. I'll see you at the Christmas planning meeting tonight. Seven-thirty, is it?'

On receiving confirmation, Bear excused himself and wondered why he had acted on impulse and changed his plans for the evening.

Chapter Eight
Valuation and Assembly

'An interesting design,' observed Hugo Chisholm in a non-committal way, as he surveyed the piece presented to him. 'Where did you get it? Or is it a family heirloom?'

It had been a long morning and the free valuation session at Blake's Auctioneers had dragged somewhat. There had been several customers directed his way to receive a consultation in his area of expertise, jewellery and metalwork. He reflected that he often started his short interviews with clients in the same way. He confessed that sometimes he was feigning interest, knowing that some had travelled a distance on a Saturday morning to have their items looked at and for him to cast his expert eye over them and, it was hoped, announce that he was gazing at an object of rare value. Such instances were exceptional, however, and Hugo was often obliged to let the customer down gently, saying the article was unlikely to fetch a significant price, but 'you never know'. Hugo, dressed in a light brown tweed jacket, beige cravat and crushed strawberry corduroys, was the epitome of a country gentleman. An amiable man in his early sixties, he had spent a lifetime in the antiques trade and generally enjoyed these Saturday consultations, although he knew the likelihood of a genuine find was remote.

What was probably going to be the last customer of the

morning had travelled up to the auction rooms in Norwich slightly flustered. He had made his way through dense traffic and struggled to find a parking space after his protracted journey from Princewood. Having been assigned a ticket and asked to wait in a queue for the relevant expert, it was a good three quarters of an hour before the customer was able to step forward to present his piece for inspection. This was not the way he had intended to spend a rare free Saturday, and the few minutes he would have to discuss with the expert hardly seemed to justify the stress of the morning's venture.

Hugo was similarly keen to afford his last customer no more than a polite audience, a few knowing remarks and words of encouragement, and set off home for lunch. He sensed, however, that there was a determined edge to his client, and steeled himself for a more extensive discussion.

'I bought it at a market in Portugal this summer,' the customer replied. Realising that a more thorough answer should be forthcoming, he added, 'I bought it for my aunt and was thinking of giving it to her for Christmas. I was intrigued by the design, and I thought I'd better check it out further, just in case it's worth more than I thought.'

Bear hated lying, or even, in the current parlance, being 'economical with the truth'. He did not want to go into a convoluted story of how he came to be in possession of someone else's property and was still guarding it several weeks after its purchase. Having to explain the amazing coincidence of meeting Sophie and arranging to hand the brooch back to her in a few weeks' time seemed far-fetched and the aunt story seemed his best cover.

'Do you know anything about the design?' probed Hugo in an engaging tone that suggested that he was excited by the object and poised to answer his own question authoritatively. In fact, he was eager to gain a few seconds to choose his words carefully.

'I gather that equestrian motifs were quite common in Iberia in the seventeenth century,' Bear replied, drawing on his knowledge from the snatched few minutes of the television documentary a few weeks previous.

'That's right,' Hugo confirmed, 'but it's not that common. The motif was widespread only among certain noble families at the time; it was almost like a coat of arms and the brooch would often be one of a set.'

Bear's ears pricked up at this detail. 'A set? So there could be other brooches out there like this one?'

'Not impossible, if they have survived. I do know that only someone of considerable standing in society would own such an item.'

'Really? Wouldn't it be in gold in that case?'

'Not necessarily. The real value lies in the uniqueness and intricacy of the individual designs. One Portuguese nobleman had had flowers of the region exquisitely carved into a set of brooches. Only one has survived, to my knowledge, but raised a tidy sum at auction a few years ago, if I recall.'

'I suppose the question is, is it genuine? And if so, are there other similar brooches out there?'

'That is a question I could not answer right away,' mused Hugo. After a few minutes' chat on the history of the Iberian Peninsula, including cultural tastes prevalent in the region at the time, it was natural for Bear to reveal his profession. Polite small talk concerning historical matters and the teaching of history today briefly alleviated a growing tension in the air. It was clear to Bear that the expert was loath to dismiss him with best wishes for whatever Bear chose to do with the item, that Hugo was searching for an excuse to prolong the discussion.

'I could… if you wish… investigate further. I could take the item along to a specialist in this period who should be able to provide a definitive answer,' Hugo carefully suggested. 'I would, of course, sign a document to confirm that it is in the temporary hands of Blake's Auctioneers. Would that be a helpful way forward?'

Given the undisclosed reason why Bear was not in any position to relinquish, even temporarily, an item that did not belong to him, it was inevitable that the offer was politely declined. With no further discussion likely to be forthcoming, Bear decided to push the expert for a figure.

'If this brooch proves to be one of a set from a Spanish or Portuguese noble, what would it be worth at auction?'

Hugo edged forward in his seat to address his questioner and lowered his voice significantly. 'It's a big "if", you understand, but if genuine….'

The next sentence left Bear's head reeling as he headed back to Princewood that afternoon, at one point electing to head into a lay-by to ponder the significance of the potential finding. He was barely aware of the blaring horn of an irate driver behind him who understandably took exception to Bear's very late decision to indicate that he intended to leave the road.

* * * *

The following week began quietly for Bear, for which he was thankful. The initial report on the inspection had been favourable, concerning the quality of instruction and administration provided by the school and the effectiveness of the pastoral care system in place for Princewood's pupils. Colleagues were generally relaxed and settling to their routines after the demands of the visit of the inspectors. Bear had barely touched base with Rob on the Monday, learning that the Under-16A team had maintained their unbeaten start to the season. This was no surprise to Bear as the opponents, Sidworth, could only field one team per age group and struggled to muster a full complement on occasion. Bear's major concern for the week was preparation for an assembly that he was due to conduct the following Tuesday. It was a duty he was looking forward to, but one that was not without its potential hazards.

Each staff member was required to take an assembly at least twice a year. This requirement usually involved being responsible for one junior, and one senior assembly at some stage in the academic year. The teacher in question would announce a hymn, read out any notices for the day and give a short talk, finishing up with a closing prayer. The more enterprising members of staff would organise a more interactive affair and involve pupils in creating a little sketch. Others would simply complete a speech for the ten minutes available. Bear's method was somewhere in the middle of the spectrum. He liked to get pupils involved, and for the junior assembly, that worked perfectly as he could invite members of his tutor group to participate. It was the junior assembly that loomed, and he mentioned at registration that Monday morning that he was looking for volunteers—two boys, two girls—to read part of the story of a famous person's life. He did not want to give away the entire details of the person concerned, so he restricted the explanation to saying it was someone who helped save other people's lives.

Enough hands were raised to offer to read, partly in the knowledge that 'house points' would inevitably be awarded for participation in a public gathering. Bear made his selection, promising others would be chosen for the next time he was organising something, he had vaguely added. A rendezvous was decided upon for an initial rehearsal after lunch that day.

* * * *

'So, how are preparations going for the other Princewood?' Bear asked cheerily as he occupied a seat next to Alan Cartwright at breaktime the following day.

'Getting there,' Alan replied. 'There was one German pupil who had to pull out for family reasons, but they quickly found a replacement and our student seems happy with it, so barring any late dramas, all set to go.'

The other Princewood, to which Bear referred, was the town of Fürstenwald in northern Bavaria, with which Princewood had an exchange link with a secondary school, the Ernst Keller Gymnasium. Each year a party of some twenty students from Suffolk headed to Germany in the autumn on the first leg of an exchange visit, reciprocating hospitality the following spring for their German partners. It had been a source of amusement to the local press when the connection had been established some eight years previously that the towns' names meant exactly the same in both languages. Indeed, the mayor of Princewood was left scratching his head, wondering why a twinning link had never been set up before. A lack of initiative, Alan concluded, when asked about it. This was in marked contrast to the almost evangelical zeal of the exchange's founder, Franz Baumann, who deliberately targeted Princewood School as a possible partner school for exchanges and won over both the headmaster and the Modern Languages Department with his charm and enthusiasm. The exchange was set up with the proviso that the first leg of the exchange should be in Bavaria (officially, the German-speaking part of the exchange) as Alan knew that if English was spoken exclusively from the start, given the superior linguistic ability of most of the German participants, very little German would be practised in the spring. In practice, it was always a battle to persuade the German hosts to refrain from using English to explain difficulties, but at least the arrangement had a semblance of a plan to maximise linguistic skills.

Bear's interest was not one of mere polite enquiry. He had the pleasure of accompanying the group the previous year as a late replacement, when a freak accident resulted in Alan's fellow Germanist Paul Slater breaking his arm and being rendered unable to travel. At a fortnight's notice Bear had agreed to step in, for which Alan and his Modern Languages colleagues were immensely grateful. Blessed with one year's schoolboy German and heavily reliant on Alan for communication, Bear nevertheless warmed to the experience. The fact that Fürstenwald was located just seven kilometres south of the former border with the German Democratic Republic was a fascination to him. The bizarre experience of travelling in a north-westerly direction on a day trip into the former East Germany, stopping at a former border post on the way, had been fuel for subsequent classroom and pub anecdotes. The sombre explanation at that point of the German school's history teacher, Herr Schreiner, that 'here the world came to an end' was indelibly marked on Bear's memory.

After asking Alan to pass on greetings to colleagues he had met in Germany the year before, Bear ascertained when the party was due to leave for Bavaria.

'Four o'clock, Sunday morning, the day after we break up on Saturday week,' Alan replied with the nonchalance of a seasoned traveller on educational visits, used to early starts. 'By the way, I heard some strange Germanic sounds coming from your classroom while I was doing the rounds on duty after lunch yesterday.'

Bear looked puzzled initially, then realised to what Alan was referring.

'Oh, you must mean the rehearsal for my Dietrich Bonhoeffer assembly next week. Probably my lousy German pronunciation. Actually, if I can catch you to work out how to say a few names, that would be helpful.'

'Sure thing. Not that a few unorthodox vowels will lessen the impact of the occasion, I'm sure.'

'No, but it helps to be as accurate as possible. Mind you, it's not just the German sounds that concern me. The one thing I am worried about is getting Daniel Walker to say "persecution" properly.'

'Ah well, Bear, if you must use long words… they have to walk before they can run, you know…'

'Well, after three attempts he kept saying "prosecution" instead of "persecution". He is going to read a passage about Bonhoeffer working to get Jews out of Germany into Switzerland during the Second World War. He reads beautifully until he gets to that point, but for some reason, whenever he should say "persecution", he gets it wrong. If he says, "the prosecution of the Jews", I fear there will be too much laughter in the hall that will hardly be appropriate. I might have to get someone else to read it to be on the safe side.'

'No need to do that. It wouldn't matter even if dear Daniel does get it wrong,' commented Alan confidently.

'Why ever not?'

'Because the word for persecution and prosecution in German is the same—*Verfolgung*. They mean the same thing to a German. It would add to the irony if the two words were confused. Makes you think, though, how a lack of distinction in two words can say a lot about such a regime? Just one short step from bullying and harassment to condemning a whole race.'

'Hmm… thank you for that, Alan. A weighty thought for a lower-school assembly. I might consider including your observation next week.'

'As you wish. Hope the assembly goes well,' replied the German specialist, rising to his feet to replace his coffee cup, tapping Bear chummily on the shoulder. Bear reflected with an amused smile to himself that he imagined some of the rugby matches Alan refereed must go into considerable injury time if he had to pause to impart to the players an interesting comment on the vagaries of the laws of the game.

In the event the assembly passed off remarkably smoothly. After the opening hymn Bear waited briefly for the gathering of eleven- to fourteen-year-olds, about a third of the school, to settle into their seats before striding to the lectern and beginning with a rhetorical question.

'I wonder how many of you have felt compelled to do something that you knew was the right thing to do but also felt it made no sense at all?' Bear let the question hang in the air before introducing the topic for the morning, the life of the famous pastor and theologian, Dietrich Bonhoeffer.

Thereupon he invited his four readers to tell something of the life of Bonhoeffer, of his origins in a respectable middle-class German family at the beginning of the twentieth century, the experience gained abroad in pastorates in Barcelona and London, and opposition to the Nazi regime when Hitler came to power. A fifth student skilfully placed acetate slides on the overhead projector to depict Bonhoeffer himself, his associates and a map of Europe at the time. Bear had left the detail he most wanted to emphasise to Charlotte Smart, the strongest and most expressive of his quartet of readers. Clearly, and with appropriate stress and pace, she recounted the dilemma Bonhoeffer faced in the summer of 1939. Having secured an academic post in the United States that would keep him away from the horrors of the approaching war in Europe, he wrestled with his conscience and had found it impossible to take up the position. How could he, Charlotte emphasised with the passion of a barrister appealing to a jury, be a part of rebuilding any new Germany after the war if he had stayed away in her hour of need? Bonhoeffer resigned his new post before starting it and sailed back from New York to Hamburg in August 1939, just before the war started and further transatlantic crossings were suspended. Any concern Bear may have had that the drama would recede as the baton passed on to Daniel Walker was swiftly dispelled as the student carefully pronounced his line about the 'persecution of the Jews' and related how Bonhoeffer had worked undercover helping Jews escape to Switzerland. At that point Bear himself concluded the story with the details of Bonhoeffer's arrest and eventual execution in April 1945, just days before Germany surrendered.

The stage was set for Bear's thought-provoking question. Those in the audience who had been taught by him were almost anticipating the challenge. Others, less familiar with Bear's style of delivery, listened intensely, eager to discover how the teacher would bring the presentation to a dénouement. Bear surveyed the assembled ranks of a hundred and fifty students and accompanying teachers before delivering his telling blow.

'What would you have done in the summer of 1939 when you knew that you had to return to Germany, even though it was likely you might not survive the war? Bonhoeffer could have opted for a safe life in the United States. You will see movies where the hero gets out of a disaster area just in the nick of time, He entered the lions' den just in the nick of time. Was he right? Maybe the people we should be asking are the Jews he helped escape, some of whom are still alive today.' Bear paused to allow time for reflection before adding, 'Let us pray.' He concluded the proceedings with a prayer about making the right decisions and following the voice of conscience, even at the cost of one's personal comfort. Little did Bear know, as he heaved a sigh of relief at the conclusion of the assembly and congratulated his pupils on their contributions, that this theme would recur several times over the following weeks.

Chapter Nine
Camden

As she glanced at her watch for the fifth or sixth time that hour, Sophie began to feel misgivings about the encounter that was about to take place. She had arrived at Camden Market a few minutes before four o'clock that Saturday afternoon in late October and enjoyed a preliminary stroll around a few of her favourite stalls. She was no stranger to the famous market and in the two years that she had been living in the district had made several purchases for herself and others. It was here that she had arranged to meet Bear to enable him finally to hand her the brooch that he had been involuntarily looking after for several weeks. Bear had informed her that he was cat-sitting for his sister in Surrey throughout the half-term break and could meet Sophie in town during the week. That was impossible, she regretted, as she was out of town on sales business every day as most of the state schools on her patch had not broken up yet and several visits were planned. With no obvious solution presenting itself, Sophie suggested meeting at Camden Market ('a chance for some early Christmas shopping', she cheerfully suggested, to which Bear had responded with a mock groan). She added that they could go on to dinner somewhere, echoing Bear's tentative proposal earlier in the week. On an impulse she had added, 'And it's my treat. It's the least I can do after you have guarded my jewellery for so long.'

She had immediately wondered if that was a wise suggestion; if the evening went well, in Bear's estimation but not hers, he would be obliged to offer to reciprocate and she might find it difficult to refuse. Yet something told her that she had nothing to worry about. They would have plenty to talk about after their humorous reunion at Princewood, he would hand over the brooch, they would enjoy a nice meal, part company amicably and that would be that. It wasn't as if they were going on a date, after all. After Bear's half-hearted questioning ('Are you sure?'), he had graciously accepted the offer and agreed to meet her at a designated point at four o'clock that afternoon.

It had been a curious half-term week for Bear. He had not lingered long after the fixtures the previous Saturday. His team had been soundly beaten, not unexpectedly, by Templefields College, a well-drilled outfit from a boarding school in Cambridgeshire. So, more surprisingly, had Mac's team, who had dismally failed to reach expectations and surrendered their hitherto unbeaten record. The half-term break meant the inquest into the defeat would be postponed for the players, and possibly tempered and rationalised by the passage of time. Not so for Bear, who had agreed to meet up with his friend one evening at a West End pub and not surprisingly had to endure a good twenty minutes' lament on the shortcomings of the Under-16A team.

Otherwise it had been a relaxing, if frustrating week for Bear. He enjoyed having the run of his sister's house and looking after the family's black cat Reiver. He had made a couple of other trips into London apart from meeting up with Mac and taken in visits to the National Film Theatre, bookshops and the Victoria and Albert Museum. He had enjoyed the ambience but was disappointed from the outset that he would have to wait until Saturday before finally being unburdened of the brooch. Nevertheless, he was looking forward to meeting Sophie again, especially now that he had an albeit unconfirmed valuation to impart, courtesy of Hugo Chisholm. He had not dared tell her of his visit to Blake's nor Hugo's verdict in the unlikely event that he might mislay the item before seeing her.

As he descended the steps of Morden station, the southern terminus of the Northern Line of the London Underground, Bear was once more in reflective mood. Whilst the week had been largely uneventful thus far, he experienced a warm sense of satisfaction in having carried out his duties as uncle and cat-sitter. He had arrived late on Saturday evening to be greeted by his older sister Angela and her husband Martin. They were pleased that they had not had to wait up for him, although their children, twelve-year-old Mark and his nine-year-old sister Emma had gone to bed. Bear had had to remain at school for social formalities following his team's fixture before making the laborious journey around the capital on London's outer orbital road. He was slightly in awe of his sister, who, having married Martin shortly after they had both left university, had entered the job market only after Emma's fifth birthday. Angela had taken a teaching post in a primary school in what was considered one of the tougher districts of south London and had quickly made her mark with a regime of compassion mingled with clear guidelines and firm discipline. In under three years she had risen to the role of deputy head. She was an extremely organised person, with precise instructions ready to deliver to her younger brother for his stay.

Martin, by contrast, was tall, thin, unassuming, giving a deceptive air of laissez-faire casualness. In fact, he was a diligent accountant with a city firm and much respected in his field. Bear almost expected a regular self-deprecating comment from Martin about being only a 'boring' figures man, but he was far from boring, with a wide general knowledge that had been invaluable in many a pub quiz and a broad range of conversation that suggested he did not spend all his day buried in statistics.

Once Angela had been satisfied that her younger brother had understood instructions for any eventualities that might arise during their absence, she and Martin retired to catch up on some sleep before their well-earned half-term week in Menorca. Bear confirmed that he would be up at five o'clock to see them off as he knew the children would insist on waking him anyway. Sure enough, he had scarcely donned his dressing gown before Mark and Emma burst into the guest room.

'Uncle Bear! Bear hugs!' they cried in unison.

Bear responded with a firm embrace of the pair of them. His brief enquiries about their health and wishes that they had a really exciting holiday were almost ritualistically cut short by a request for Bear to take his place in goal. On many a visit, Bear had acted as goalkeeper in front of the football goal erected at the bottom of the garden. He had enjoyed playing dead after seizing the ball to complete a miraculous save before being jumped upon by the children in an affectionate embrace. Angela, anticipating this request, was firm. Five in the morning was not the time to disturb the neighbours' suburban slumber with such noisy activity, especially with a plane to catch. Bear consoled his nephew and niece with a promise to resume custodial duties on their return.

Having waved off the Balearics-bound party, Bear was left to attend to Reiver. Ah, Reiver. Now that was a story, he mused as he boarded the northbound train towards Camden Town. When Mark and Emma were distraught and inconsolable at the demise of the family tabby Jemima two years previously, the children were asked if they had any thoughts on naming a possible successor. As Bear had looked after Jemima on several occasions, the children were happy to defer the choice of name to their uncle who was due to visit the following day. On seeing the six-month old black feline boldly exploring room after room, Bear named him 'Reiver' after the infamous Anglo-Scottish Border Reivers (or raiders) who used to raid the border country in the summer months in centuries gone by. It was not long before Reiver set about living up to his name, terrorising the mouse population of suburban Surrey. That week had seen two further 'offerings' gleefully exhibited to the stand-in cat-parent on Martin and Angela's back patio.

Bear's reveries were cut short as he realised his journey was completed and he made his way up flights of escalators to the surface. Having looked forward to meeting up with Sophie and being delivered of his burden, he felt a twinge of nervousness. He sensed that he might have triggered an involuntary, yet outwardly confident, invitation to dinner, and wondered whether conversation that had been so free-flowing in Valença do Minho in the summer could be comfortably sustained away from the carefree holiday atmosphere. He was also worried, however, about having to broach the subject of the brooch's worth to Sophie. Momentarily smiling at the unintended pun on 'brooch', he considered deploying the witticism in conversation with Sophie later, but quickly dismissed the idea as he was unsure whether she was receptive to such verbal gymnastics. He would have to choose his moment to announce Hugo's opinion and almost felt a responsibility in ensuring that no further mishaps befell the piece of jewellery while he was present.

After alighting from the station and adjusting his eyes to the light of strong late October sunshine, Bear made his way around the corner to the entrance to Camden Market. He quickly identified the prominent entrance sign displayed between buildings either side of the walkway and directed his steps immediately to the clock tower as pre-arranged. Within seconds of stopping to peruse the scene, he noticed a familiar figure casually looking at a stall turn, as though sensing his presence, and smile in his direction. Sophie exuded the same confident bearing he had observed at the café in Valença some weeks previously. The thought occurred to him that here was a person at ease with engaging with relative strangers to pass the time of day on a Saturday afternoon. She was smartly dressed in a beige jacket, delicate checked blouse and aubergine cords. Here was someone at home with the atmosphere of buying and selling, as you would expect from a saleswoman.

'Hello,' she said, smiling warmly.

'Hello,' replied Bear. 'We meet again at last,' he added, delivering his pre-rehearsed line.

'And you're punctual. Bang on four o'clock,' she responded, glancing slightly theatrically at her watch, 'I am impressed.'

'Well, I spend my working life looking at my watch, telling kids to get to lessons on time and dividing up each lesson into segments, so I should be… punctual, that is,' Bear clarified nervously, concerned that he might be rambling on.

'You've not been to Camden Market before, have you?' Sophie said, at which Bear shook his head and smiled. 'I need to give you a guided tour. This is a treasure trove you must get to know.'

'Sounds good,' Bear responded enthusiastically, although shopping was never one of his favourite activities. He braced himself for what he expected to be a tedious stroll through busy market stalls examining items that he had no interest in buying. 'But first…' he added, 'I need to finally free myself of a certain burden that belongs to you.'

Bear reached into his inside jacket pocket and produced a folded padded bag. With an exaggerated flourish he handed the package to Sophie, declaring, 'Mission accomplished, I hope.'

Sophie smiled warily at Bear as though suspicious as to the contents and carefully removed the object therein. She withdrew the long-awaited bronze brooch and surveyed it, greeting it with a warm grin.

'Hello, old friend. Sorry to leave you behind. Just as well there was an alert bear in the woods to save the day.'

Bear stood quietly, wondering whether Sophie was intending to savour the moment any longer when she abruptly announced, 'The least I can do is wear it.'

Carefully releasing the catch, she placed the item on her jacket lapel where it stood out impressively against the beige background.

'Thank you again for taking care of it,' she said, not for the first time. 'I'm sorry I was so scatty back in the summer.'

'No, I'm sorry it took so long to get it to you,' Bear replied and was about to elaborate when he realised that the mutual apologising society had reappeared and he curtailed its activities immediately.

'Let me show you the market,' said Sophie, 'that is, if you're interested?'

'Absolutely,' Bear answered, not wholly sincerely as he braced himself for a shopping saunter.

For the next half-hour they strolled from stall to stall, stopping occasionally. Sophie pointed to a plaque which indicated that the market had been operational since 1974 and now was a diverse community of creative sellers in a historic central London location. Bear found himself surprisingly drawn to the array of merchandise on offer, although not sufficiently attracted to make a purchase. In addition to the usual food and drink stalls, there were some items of clothing that drew Sophie's attention, and for a few minutes she surveyed a stall selling jewellery and other metal ware objects. It was at a table where wooden handiwork was on offer that she lingered the most. Bear, for once, was impressed by the carvings of various birds and was distracted for a few minutes, thinking that one could possibly find a home on Angela and Martin's mantelpiece. It was while Sophie was struggling to make sense of a wooden gadget that looked like an abacus but designed as a children's toy and seemed amused at working out its functions that Bear looked up to notice a tall, dark-haired man with a swarthy, perhaps Mediterranean complexion looking intently in her direction. That's odd, he thought, but did not comment as he was several feet away at the other end of the table. He resumed his rummage through carved birds but was then aware of a conversation developing to his left.

'Where did you get it?' a thick male voice in a southern European accent was heard to ask.

'Oh, on holiday in Portugal,' Sophie responded cheerily.

'Really? I am from Portugal. Where was that?'

Sophie politely informed the stranger of the visit to the market in the border town that summer, being economic with the details, as if to say that it was not the time or the place for a lengthy chat. Her interlocutor, however, was equally polite but gently persistent. He was impressed, he claimed, at the craftsmanship of the workers in bronze in Iberia in centuries past. Sophie agreed unconvincingly and turned to notice Bear, who abandoned his perusal of things avian and drew close to enquire.

'It seems my brooch has more admirers,' she said, pointing to the stranger. 'This gentleman is from Portugal.'

'Oh yes? Whereabouts?' Bear asked but immediately regretted the question.

The enquiry gave the stranger licence to talk of his region, slightly to the east and south of where the pair had met and of how he was enjoying his stay in London. Bear and Sophie listened politely, although Bear was starting to grow restless with the Portuguese's bonhomie. Sophie continued to smile as she listened with sparing comment to remarks on the culture, geography and history of the Minho region, observations about differences between Portuguese and British culture and what amused him most during his occasional visits to London. It was this last point that brought the rather one-sided conversation to a head. It seemed natural for Sophie to ask the inevitable question.

'So what brings you to London?'

'I deal in antiques,' the tall stranger replied, 'I specialise in wood and metalwork. I often come to markets like this. Listen, I'm sure your time is precious, so I'll come straight to the point.' Bear smiled to himself; ten minutes' ramble on cultural differences hardly constituted 'coming straight to the point' in his book.

'I collect antiques that have a common theme, and your brooch would fit in very well with my collection. In fact, it would be an essential part,' the Portuguese continued, emphasising the word 'essential'. 'Could I buy it off you? How much would you accept for it? I have a hundred pounds in cash on me.'

Sophie was taken aback at the stranger's directness and the fact that she had received an offer to sell the item of jewellery within minutes of wearing it for the first time. She turned to Bear for support, and he immediately countered,

'You must be joking. It's worth much more than that!'

The offer was promptly doubled. 'Two hundred then.' There was an earnestness, even pleading in the Portuguese's eyes. To Bear's horror, it looked as if Sophie was wavering.

'It's not for sale, is it, Sophie?' he asked, but more as a statement of intent than a question.

'No, sorry,' she said, shaking her head at the stranger, 'but thank you for your interest. And good luck in the rest of your visit.'

The man smiled sadly as instinctively, Bear and Sophie headed away from the stall towards the exit. They were silent for a few seconds, keen to put some distance between themselves and the unusual encounter.

Finally, Sophie suggested, 'Is it time for a cup of tea?'

'I somehow think on this occasion I could do with something stronger. Are there any decent pubs around here?'

They exited the market, turned around a couple of corners and alighted upon a quiet pub in one of the side streets. They entered and were pleased to note that it was still relatively empty, it being late afternoon and before the influx of early-evening drinkers. Bear offered to buy the drinks as he knew Sophie had insisted on buying dinner, headed to the bar and returned to join Sophie at seats at the back of the bar with a glass of white wine for her and a pint of beer for himself. Sophie began to initiate conversation about Bear's half-term, and his initial agitation about the encounter in the market started to dissipate as he talked of his evening with Mac and shared of their friendship and common coaching exploits. She seemed genuinely interested and in return talked of the characters in her sales team, especially Max's quirky humour, and how they jollied one another along through thick and thin times.

After twenty minutes or so, the pair of them had visibly relaxed and were enjoying the early evening when a familiar figure entered the room to their left. The pub was still sufficiently empty for them naturally to glance at the newcomer, and recognition was inevitable.

'Hello! We meet again. What a surprise!' exclaimed the Portuguese antique dealer.

'Yes, isn't it?' Sophie responded, smiling politely. Bear nodded at the stranger in acknowledgement but was clearly not looking forward to a resumption of their earlier conversation. The dealer, uninvited, occupied a vacant seat at the round table where the pair were seated. Bear had a strong suspicion that they had been followed.

'May I ask if you have had any more thoughts on selling the brooch? Forgive me, but where I come from, we can be very direct. Perhaps it is no coincidence that we have met again.'

'If you're that keen,' Bear interrupted before Sophie could answer, 'you must know that it's worth much more than a couple of hundred.'

'Possibly,' the Portuguese replied with a non-committal shrug of the shoulders. 'How about three hundred? It would mean a lot to me.' He looked at Sophie intently, as if soliciting a sympathetic response from someone who understood the importance of securing a key deal.

Perhaps he realised that she was in the sales business, thought Bear.

Sophie reflected for a moment, then directed her gaze back at the dealer. 'No, sorry. It's not for sale,' she said firmly. Bear breathed a sigh of relief.

'Well, if you change your mind...' the dealer said, reaching into his wallet, 'it's really important to...'

'Look,' Bear intervened, rather more forcibly than he wanted, 'she said she's not interested and that's the end of it. I think you should go, mate.'

'Okay, okay,' retorted the Portuguese, raising both hands in mock surrender. He rose to his feet and placed two business cards on the table, not the wad of cash that Bear had anticipated. 'If you do change your mind, my name is Pedro. My hotel number in London is in the back. I will return to Portugal on Tuesday.'

With that he nodded to the pair and swiftly left the pub. It was a few seconds before either of them spoke. When conversation did resume, they were both at a loss to work out why Pedro had been so persistent, even desperate to make the purchase. Sophie felt admiration for Pedro's tenacity, remembering she often had to be similarly determined to secure sales, but she was also curiously touched by his earnest pleading. Though he did not care to admit it then, Bear was also stirred by the dealer's entreaties.

It was not until later in the evening that Bear felt able to deliver the bombshell he had been concealing. Sophie decided that a change of atmosphere was called for, and suggested heading to a favourite Italian restaurant she had selected for the promised meal. Bear agreed to drink up and move on, reasoning that they were much less likely to be pestered a third time in the more formal setting of the restaurant than in the convivial, casual atmosphere of a pub. Once they had settled at their table at Gorgio's and had their glasses charged with Tuscan white wine, Bear proposed a toast to chance encounters at Portuguese border towns. Sophie smiled. They clinked glasses and sampled the wine while they waited for their food order to arrive.

'I can't think why this Pedro was so desperate to buy the brooch,' Sophie said. 'I mean, most people would have given up after I turned him down at the market.'

'I have a good idea,' responded Bear.

'What do you mean?'

'I mean I have reason to believe it's worth a lot more than what he offered for it.'

'How do you know that?'

'I think you'd better put your glass down for a moment. I need to prepare you for a shock.'

Sophie did as Bear requested. He told her of his meeting with Hugo Chisholm and the estimated value of the brooch.

'What!' she exclaimed, her voice increasing in volume. 'Twenty…' She then corrected herself to lower her voice to a whisper. 'Twenty thousand pounds?'

'At least. If it is part of a set, then possibly much more.'

'So that was why you were so keen for me not to part with it.'

'Exactly. It's your choice, of course, but the question is… do you plan to keep it now you have some idea of its true value?'

The question hung in the air as a reflective silence gripped the atmosphere, conveniently punctuated by the arrival of the dishes ordered. It was a matter that proved unsurprisingly dominant in their conversation as the evening progressed but remained unresolved as they parted ways two hours later.

Chapter Ten
Revelation

Emily Richards had found the opening fifteen minutes of her first quarterly sales team meeting relatively easy to follow, and she was feeling increasingly comfortable in her surroundings. That morning in early November, each member of the team was present at the head office of Foundation Books in north London to report on recent sales, success or otherwise of marketing strategies, trends spotted while on sales visits and ideas for improving future sales. The senior member of each geographical division of the Foundation Books (Education Department) Sales Team, to give its full title, was required to deliver a report on the last three months' sales. In her case, Ryan, being responsible for East Anglia, reported on progress up to the end of October.

Naturally, he acknowledged that because of his incapacity, Sophie had taken over for a few weeks and thanked her for covering for him. He was also very complimentary of Emily for her enthusiasm, engagement with customers and no little knowledge acquired in a very short space of time. Other senior sales reps, including Sophie, delivered their reports, supported by handouts of figures and charts, and the general picture seemed to be positive with clear areas of growth, but also some frustrations and setbacks. Emily enjoyed imbibing the dynamism and optimism of the atmosphere and was starting to feel very much in her element and enjoying the camaraderie of the company and its confident, outgoing emphasis.

Foundation Books had advanced steadily from humble beginnings in the mid-nineteenth century. The brainchild of a Victorian philanthropist, it had been set up as a publisher, initially of small, eight-page pamphlets designed to teach the fundamentals (hence the name 'Foundation') of reading, writing and arithmetic to poorer children in the East End of London. After initial success throughout much of the capital, the company had broadened its range to publish textbooks on a range of subjects in primary education. In the years following the First World War, further expansion into secondary education had followed, with talented authors attracted to the brand. Wider diversification had seen the establishment of the Travel Books section in the 1970s and a smaller, but growing Non-fiction section for adults had emerged around the same time. The Education Department was still the largest of the three sections, with a sales team of fifteen operating in London and the south-east, and smaller teams in the Midlands and the north-west. An office in Glasgow had recently been mooted with the aim of establishing a foothold in Scotland. When her friends had heard that Emily had accepted a job in sales, the reaction had been that training would inevitably be crude and rudimentary, but in fact the course had been thoughtfully prepared, showing precise knowledge of the market and interests and needs of educational professionals. After two months with Foundation Books, she dared to say to herself, she was starting to feel at home.

Her sense of comfort was jolted somewhat, however, when Max Chandler, having received the regional reports, stood up to speak. He switched on the overhead projector, inserted an acetate showing a bar chart to depict overall sales and began to speak. Within a matter of seconds Emily found herself turning around to her colleagues with a quizzical glance.

Sophie was not slow to pick up on her younger colleague's confusion. Max had just explained that, whilst sales of publications on teachers' motivational strategies had been reasonable, they had been 'beaten to the punch' by the government-sponsored CanDo Foundation in several areas. The astute Dr Pamela Simpson had been combing the country with her team, delivering workshops and selling multiple copies of one significant work, *Can't is a four-letter word*, which seemed to have a clear edge over Foundation Books' *Doing It My Way—motivational strategies for teachers*, much to the frustration of the sales management.

'In various places, we got in after the horse had bolted, and it was a case of tooly toolah, I'm afraid,' Max lamented.

Emily turned to Sophie open-mouthed, trying to work out what department or trade lingo she had missed out on in her training. Sophie was moved to intervene but not before Max continued his summative judgement.

'So we can carry on pushing *Doing It My Way*, folks, but it look like it's going to be dam-lim for a while on that one.'

This time Sophie felt she could not avoid interrupting.

'Excuse me, Max, but I think you need to translate some of your terms.'

'What's that, Soph?' Max queried, seemingly puzzled to have his flow interrupted.

'I'm not sure Emily is familiar with some of your expressions.'

'Oh, sorry, Em. What's not clear?'

'Well, I…' Emily began, but Sophie intervened to speed up proceedings.

'"Tooly toolah" in English means "too little, too late".'

'I see. And what was the other one… dam…?'

'"Dam lim". Otherwise known as "damage limitation". Don't worry, there's more where they come from,' Sophie added, raising an eyebrow.

Emily smiled gratefully, though somewhat bemused by this sudden influx of new language. The initiation had not quite finished, however.

'So we need to find some way of countering Doctor Pam,' Max continued, 'otherwise we may struggle to get our…' He paused theatrically, looking up to the team, who with the exception of Emily, responded as required.

'… munbows!' they exclaimed, some more heartily than others.

'Monthly bonuses,' Sophie whispered to Emily.

Thankfully, there were no more of Max's neologisms for Emily to digest. The course of the meeting turned to a discussion of ways to combat the infiltration of the CanDo Foundation. It turned out that three other colleagues representing different areas of the south-east of England had visited schools and colleges where a Dr Pamela workshop had preceded them. Sales of *Doing It My Way* had been unspectacular, but hardly disastrous. Evidence gathered thus far, albeit anecdotal, was that Foundation Books' latest motivational publication might yet prove a significant success. Sophie was able to add her second-hand contribution, saying that a teacher she was talking to in Suffolk informed her that one of his colleagues had bought both the discussed publications. Rob McAllister would doubtless have been amused to know that he was the subject of earnest deliberations of a national educational bookseller. The anecdotes turned into a debate as to whether Doctor Pam, as Max called her, specialised more in precise examples of affirmative language, while Maurice Painter (alias Little Mo), author of *Doing It My Way*, explored more in-depth strategies to motivate teachers, and by extension, their pupils. It was at this point that Catherine Holdsworth, the most experienced member of the sales team with a wealth of experience in the education field, interjected to suggest that it would be a good idea if Foundation Books steered away from sounding combative towards the CanDo Foundation and offered themselves as a complement to Dr Simpson's undoubted success. It would do no harm, Catherine maintained, to be seen unofficially as partners in the motivational processes in the classroom, and while CanDo's bubble was yet to burst, subtle association with, and endorsement of another company's publication could be to Foundation Books' advantage.

These thoughts were left to hang in the air for a few moments. Catherine's judgement was usually accurate, although some members of the team were sceptical as to whether overt praise of a competitor could draw buyers' attention to what they all perceived as their own Little Mo's weightier tome.

'I have read both books,' added Catherine, 'and there is nothing in Maurice's book that flatly contradicts any of Dr Simpson's linguistic strategies. I would even go as far as saying that if we encouraged sales of *Can't is a four-letter word*, we would direct attention to Maurice much more easily.'

There was an uncomfortable silence as the team digested

this view. Education sales were no different from other sales work as staff were expected to know their products. That meant reading a number of books each year. From the muted response to Catherine's observations few, if any, had got around to reading both the publications being discussed. To be fair, though, this sales team did attract graduates, those used to extensive reading and indeed, some ex-teachers. Catherine, now in her late fifties, had taught in inner London for some twenty-five years and had used her many contacts to strengthen Foundation Books' foothold in the market in north London. Sophie had graduated in geography and was motivated by a love of travel. She had often thought of asking for a transfer to the travel section of the company, but was aware that such a move would entail some demanding in-depth visits to different countries to update information, a very different proposition to breezing in for a care-free fortnight's holiday. If such an opportunity presented herself, she reasoned, it would be hard to ignore, as it would certainly make use of her abilities.

Max Chandler correctly deemed that a slightly extended coffee break was called for to give time for the team to chat about their experiences over the past three months. They trooped out of the seminar room to a neighbouring lounge where the coffee percolator was already operational. While others poured themselves a coffee, Sophie helped herself to a fruit tea and sat down at one of the sofas. Catherine Holdsworth drew up alongside her.

'Was that you I saw in Camden Market on Saturday?' she asked cheerily.

'Very possibly,' Sophie replied.

'You were talking to some tall, dark handsome stranger,'

Catherine elaborated by way of clarification with a smile of amusement before adding, 'and then another gentleman seemed to whisk you away. I must say, you seem to be in demand these days, my dear,' she winked.

'Oh... that was just a friend. The second chap, I mean,' Sophie ventured to explain awkwardly. 'The other guy was trying to sell me something.'

A few minutes of cordial conversation ensued. Sophie successfully steered Catherine away from any speculation concerning possible romantic developments towards more mundane matters. She recalled how pleased she had been to find a flat in Camden two years previously and how she enjoyed the relative anonymity of the city, having grown up in rural Devon. Throughout her childhood you couldn't breathe without the village gossips broadcasting it. Now she could pursue relationships with whom she wished, stay up to all hours, dress as garishly as she chose without fear of disapproval, or even comment, from neighbours or colleagues. Unless, she was soon to learn, she met up with Catherine. Her older colleague, she learned, lived just a few streets away and had soon taken a motherly interest in Sophie, who had been on the rebound after the break-up of a relationship when she moved to the area. Fortunately, Catherine was not one to probe and at that moment was drawn into chatter by Max who asked her opinion about some local building project.

There was a copy of *The Times* on the coffee table open at page seven. Sophie had a few minutes before the meeting was to resume, so she half-heartedly picked up the newspaper to scan the headlines to see if there was anything of interest. She soon regretted her move. The page seemed to deal with legal matters. There was a high-profile divorce settlement involving a Hollywood actress that dominated the main headline; further down the page a report that the provision of legal aid was to be debated in parliament. Neither issue grabbed Sophie's attention, and she was about to turn the page when her eye fastened on a short article at the bottom right corner of the page. Whilst the heading meant nothing to her, the sub-title caused her to read on:

EDUARDO D'OLIVEIRA ARRESTED
Jewel fraudster apprehended in northern Portugal.

What she discovered caused her a distinct sense of unease.

Portuguese police reported the arrest yesterday of Eduardo D'Oliveira, reputed to be the country's most notorious jewellery fraudster. He was tracked down in the town of Vila Real where he was staying and apprehended after a dawn raid by local police, assisted by officers from Interpol. Mr D'Oliveira, 52, is alleged to have been the mastermind behind a series of thefts and fraudulent sales of precious metal ware in the Minho region of northern Portugal. A police spokesman expressed contentment that the person considered to be responsible for extorting hundreds of people of vast sums of money had been arrested, but there was no room for complacency. There was a strong possibility, he warned, that…

Sophie read on, open-mouthed. She even re-read the article and would have done so a third time, had she not heard Ryan encouraging her to return to the seminar room for the resumption.

'Come on, Sophie. We don't want to be late for the next round of Doctor Pam versus Little Mo,' he said jovially. 'Must get our ringside seats. Can't wait to hear Susan's judgement.'

As Sophie was hesitant to respond and only slowly got to her feet, Ryan asked if she was all right.

'Yes, fine, Ryan. Won't be a minute,' she responded.

Sophie removed page seven from the newspaper, hastily headed to the photocopier and keyed in her code. She extracted the photocopied article and slipped it into her file, knowing that she would be studying it carefully later. It was not unnoticed that she was unusually quiet for the remainder of the meeting. Susan Mortimer, Head of Marketing, presented her take on the best strategy for selling *Doing It My Way*, before turning to other resources across the age ranges for educational publications. Sophie took very little in. She knew the events of the previous weekend at the market were very much a work in progress.

Chapter Eleven
Restlessness, Reinvigoration, Reflection

It would be an exaggeration to say that Bear returned reinvigorated to duties at Princewood School for the second half of term. Certainly, he had been refreshed by rest, a change of surroundings and stimulating social interaction. He had enjoyed cultural pursuits in the capital, meeting up with Mac one evening, and as ever, faithfully performing his cat-sitting duties.

Reiver was very much a 'lap cat' and was constantly jumping on to Bear's knees as he settled down to watch television. Whether the closeness was a sign of affection or appreciation for being looked after that week, or simply a desire for warmth and comfort, was unclear, although, Bear assumed, more probably the latter. Bear had enjoyed meeting Angela, Martin, Mark and Emma on the Sunday when they returned from their week in Menorca and being regaled with tales of gorgeous autumn sunshine, not-too-full beaches and exploration of the island. They were, as ever, appreciative for his care of Reiver, and remarked at how well the feline was looking. And of course, Bear had enjoyed his evening out with Sophie. He had found her pleasant company and had the impression that the feeling was reciprocated. Of course, she was a salesperson, so she was used to putting on a front, he reasoned, but there was a sense of genuine connection and ease of conversation, he felt. All things considered, it had been an agreeable half-term break, but a sense of being weighed down was inescapable.

There were two thoughts that Bear found difficult to dismiss from his mind. Firstly, the sudden emergence of Pedro Gomes at Camden Market as the third person in this drama and his 'coincidental' reappearance at the pub gave him cause for anxiety. Yes, Bear had delivered the brooch finally, as planned, and Sophie had been grateful, showing her gratitude by paying for dinner. In a sense that was the end of the matter as far as he was concerned. He had returned someone else's property that had accidentally been left in his keeping. He had been thanked for this service and even passed on information he had gathered concerning the possible value of the jewellery. End of story. End of Bear's involvement with Sophie and the brooch. Back to life in Suffolk and educating teenagers. But it was not the end of the story. He berated himself more than once at making the visit to Blake's and getting Hugo Chisholm's assessment. He now knew that the bronze brooch was worth considerably more than what Sophie paid for it, and at least one person was very keen to acquire it. Indeed, he had insisted on accompanying Sophie to her flat that Saturday evening, not out of a sense of chivalry, but just to ensure that they were not being followed. Sophie had felt compelled to say there was no need for such a precaution, but he could tell from the tone of her voice that she was not wholly convinced of what she was saying and did appreciate the need for vigilance. As it turned out, there was no sign of Pedro extending his pursuit of the item, although the earnest, almost desperate entreaties for Sophie to sell the brooch had made an impression on them both. He could not escape the notion that

129

there was more to this story than a dealer's desire to make a fast buck.

The other cause of Bear's restlessness was Sophie herself. This is ridiculous, he told himself. He could not pretend that he did not find her personality attractive. Maybe it was her more decisive, confident, sales-trained ease in engaging with people which contrasted with his more measured, thoughtful, some would say reserved, approach, but they certainly got along. That was largely down to the humorous circumstances of how they met and the unlikely reunion at Princewood, and Pedro's behaviour gave them much to discuss. Did he find her attractive in terms of pursuing a closer relationship? Perhaps. Would he like to see her again? Why not? Possibly. If the occasion arose. He wasn't sure. They had said their goodbyes at the end of the evening and exchanged pleasantries.

'If you're ever in the area, let me know…'

'And if you're selling books in Suffolk again, give me a call…' he had said, although she had told him her brief secondment to his region had finished now that Ryan was fully fit again.

So that was that. Aside from whether he wanted to meet Sophie again, he was genuinely intrigued, and not a little concerned, that she was now in possession of an item of jewellery that could be worth thousands of pounds. She needed to decide whether to keep it, and if so to look after it, or sell it on. But that was none of his business, he told himself. He had done his part, fulfilled his obligations, successfully delivered the item, the baton had been passed on, no longer his concern. Time to move on with life after an interesting episode. End of story. Case closed. Probably.

One feature of teaching, Bear reflected not for the first

time that Wednesday morning in early November, is how quickly you are obliged to forget about what has gone before and refocus, sometimes quite abruptly. He supposed it was true of most professions, but when dealing with children and their many, varied needs, there was no time to dwell on the past when new issues arose. And so it proved that morning, as his registration period involved fielding two questions by pupils, one on the procedure for a forthcoming trip and the other on an anticipated change of footwear required by someone having to see a chiropodist who was likely to advise wearing softer shoes for a period. By the time Bear had dealt with these enquiries, he had to whisk his tutor group off to assembly and thoughts of Pedro, Sophie and brooches had disappeared from his mind. Later that day, when his mind was uncluttered and able to make sense of events, he recalled a bizarre instance three years previously, when it was announced one morning on the staff notice board that a former pupil whom Bear had taught had been killed in an earthquake in Mexico while on his gap year. Bear had been about to reflect on how sad this occurrence was when he was immediately absorbed in pupil requests and three demanding lessons that followed. When he had returned to the staffroom at breaktime he had discovered an apology notice that the aforementioned ex-student was alive and well, that details had been confused and the earlier report was false. Bear, like many of his colleagues, had barely time to consider the implications of the alleged demise, let alone grieve, before the matter was declared null and void. Even the sense of relief at the false alarm was muted and felt unreal.

The re-focusing that morning took the form of a Religious Studies lesson. Wednesday, period three, was the one slot in

Bear's timetable, apart from games afternoons, not devoted to the teaching of history. At the end of the previous summer term, chaplain and head of RS Martin Bickersdike had approached him and asked if he could fill a gap teaching RS to a Year 7 class once a week. That would mean instructing the youngest pupils, eleven- to twelve-year-olds on Old Testament stories and beliefs. Bear was surprised to have been asked, never having taught the subject before. Martin confirmed that he had been informed by Roger Bulstrode, the mathematician with the unenviable task of drawing up the timetable, that with the best fit projected he was required to teach another class during that period and could anyone else fill that gap? Martin said he was sure Bear could do 'a grand job', as he had seen Bear blend scriptural references appropriately into assemblies he had conducted, and he had heard from other quarters how confident Bear was in handling stories from the Bible. Bear wondered who these 'other quarters' were, and suspected Cynthia Standish had been gushing in her praise for the few occasions when he had stood in for his midweek Bible study group leader and led discussions thoughtfully. At least, the ministers of the churches and their wives in Princewood spoke to one another, Bear thought. For one lesson per week for a year, he reasoned, he could surely help Martin, and Roger, out of a hole, and he agreed to take on the class.

So it was that 7P (so named after their form tutor, Linda Porter) trooped into Bear's classroom to begin the next in their series of lessons on Old Testament stories and beliefs. As Bear became aware of the hubbub outside the classroom, he opened the door and instructed the class to stand by a chair but not sit down yet. The class duly took up position at various points in the room with several making comments about the room looking different from their last visit.

Instead of the room being arranged in rows with tables accommodating two students each all facing the front, there were five sets of two tables and accompanying chairs arranged facing each other to form three groups of four, and two groups of five pupils, accounting for the anticipated twenty-two members of 7P. Once the class was assembled, Bear referred to his pre-arranged list and directed each pupil to a particular table to work in a specific group. That way Bear had prepared an even spread of boys and girls, a balance in intellectual ability and a mixture in each group of the quiet and the boisterous. The reason for the change from previous weeks, Bear announced, was to generate more discussion.

Bear was slightly wary of the topic for the lesson that day and had taken necessary precautions. He was required to cover the story of Jonah, the reluctant prophet who is called by God to preach to a sinful, hostile foreign city and who, when he decides to sail in the opposite direction as far away as he can, ends up being thrown overboard and swallowed by a large fish, traditionally assumed to be a whale. Whilst several in the class had already heard of the story of Jonah, none had much knowledge of the Biblical text. Bear realised that the book of Jonah, though relatively short, containing just four chapters, was nevertheless too long for a class of eleven-year-olds to read out loud, as was customary practice, at a brisk enough pace to allow for discussion and analysis at the end. So, on this occasion, he instructed the class to follow the text in their Good News Bibles while he inserted a tape into the History Department's sole cassette player and allowed a storyteller to read to the class. The actor's voice conveyed more than a modicum of awe and fascination as the events unfolded, sufficient to hold the children's attention, Bear noted with gratification. When the storyteller had reached the end of chapter one, Bear switched the tape off and addressed the class.

'In your groups I would like you to discuss the questions on chapter one and in a couple of minutes I will ask one person from each group to summarise what your answers are. Decide amongst yourselves who will report back to me on chapter one. It will be a different person for the other three chapters.'

With the pressure of time constraints, the groups began discussing earnestly what they thought of the events of the first chapter. There were just two questions to discuss: a) why did Jonah disobey God and not go to preach to the people of the wicked city of Nineveh? and b) were the sailors right to throw Jonah overboard? The second was likely to bring about the answer that they had no choice, as the storm which God had caused was only going to be stilled once the person responsible, Jonah, was ejected from the vessel. The first elicited some predictable response from the groups, with Jonah being referred to as 'scared', 'terrified', even 'lazy' and 'cowardly'. Bear repeated the procedure of playing the tape for the subsequent three chapters.

For chapter two, the class offered views on how Jonah felt while in the depths of the big fish, and what the prayer he offered tells us about his relationship with God. One fresh-faced boy raised his hand to offer a comment before Bear moved on.

'Sir, I don't think he had a whale of a time!' This remark was met with a ripple of laughter by his eleven-year-old classmates. Bear grinned sweetly; he had half-expected a similar witticism but acted as if he was hearing such an observation for the first time.

In fact, that comment served to lighten the mood, and the answers that had been safe and cautious on the first two chapters, were more searching thereafter. When Bear asked for feedback on the third pair of questions at the end of chapter three, concerning why God gave Jonah a second chance (to preach to Nineveh) and whether Jonah used his chance wisely, some lively discussion ensued that Bear had to cut short to allow time for the final chapter. Bear was gratified that there was just time for observations on chapter four, where there was broad consensus that what the final verses seemed to imply was that God's attitude to those who do wrong, in this case the people of Nineveh, was one of compassion.

Before setting the homework, Bear threw out a little teaser to the class.

'Can anyone tell me what is meant by "The sign of Jonah" that is mentioned elsewhere in the Bible?'

He was pleased that there was a sea of blank faces, which permitted him to issue his challenge.

'Right, the first person to find this expression before we next meet gets a house point, and possibly another little reward.'

Bear was glad that this class did not contain children who benefitted from churchgoing parents and either knew the answer or could find out immediately. This group would have to do their own research. He taught both of Michael and Cynthia Standish's sons, David and Andrew, both of whom would have been razor-sharp if presented with a similar poser, and the rest of their respective classes would not have had a look in. Through experience he had learned not to promise any extra prize in case some pupils profited from an unfair advantage, such as their parents' profession, which meant they had easy access to any conundrum set. On this occasion, with 7P, the genuine enquirer would be rewarded with a point for his or her house and an item of confectionary.

Bear set the fortnightly homework (being seen as a bit of a Cinderella subject, RS shared a weekly homework slot with Drama). He asked the class to write a couple of paragraphs to answer the question that he proceeded to write on the whiteboard, 'Should people always be given second chances when they get things wrong?' Bear stressed that they could refer to any religious literature they had come across or any situations in everyday life they knew about, and that it was worth considering the merits of Jonah being given a second chance when he decided to sail away to the ends of the earth to get away from his responsibilities. It was at this point that a pupil's observation gave him much cause to ponder.

'It's a bit like that German vicar, isn't it, sir?' A blonde, bespectacled boy in the nearest group remarked.

'What German vicar?' Bear asked, puzzled.

'You know, your assembly before half-term. The one who tried to escape from the Nazis, then changed his mind. I mean, they both tried to get off doing their duty by sailing away but got it right in the end.'

'Oh, you mean Dietrich Bonhoeffer... Well, I'm glad you were listening that day, Toby. Well, I'm not sure it was quite the same sort of situation...' Bear was about to say Bonhoeffer could hardly be accused of disobedience in initially taking up a university post he had been offered in the States but thought better of it. For an eleven-year-old pupil, this was a pretty astute observation and not that far off the mark. Instead Bear simply added, 'Hmm, perhaps they were rather similar, Toby.

Perhaps that's something for us all to think about.' The last sentence was addressed to the class as a cue to pack up as the lesson was ending. As he headed to the staffroom for his breaktime coffee, Bear muttered to himself thoughtfully, 'Myself included.'

The Year 7 lesson proved to be a light-hearted, stimulating highlight to what was becoming a heavy, almost oppressive Wednesday for Bear. After break, the eager innocence of discovery and questioning in the RS lesson gave way to more cynical older pupils. For some reason enthusiasm seemed in short supply in subsequent classes. Year 11, having moved away from Nazi Germany to other major world powers, were now studying the emergence of China. Mention of Mao and the Long March did not spark wonder, enquiry or admiration, but rather bemusement and sarcasm, at least among the vocal members of the group. The concept of a one-party state was now a familiar one and the arguments for the benefits of state monopoly were wearing thin on some but beginning to be championed by others. Debate, such as it was, was tetchy rather than constructive. Year 9 had progressed from the excitement of the Napoleonic Wars and embarked on the far less glamorous mid-nineteenth century and various Reform Acts. Bear's best efforts to generate a spirit of investigation met with minimal success. Even the Upper Sixth attended to the pursuit of their studies of the English Civil War with no more than dutiful care rather than thirst for learning. This can't be attributable to mid-term blues, thought Bear, we've only just got back from half-term. At least some students should be fresh and raring to go.

One obvious reason for the torpor was the fact that Princewood School had reverted to its winter timetable on the resumption of term at the beginning of that week. That meant that for three afternoons per week—Monday, Wednesday and Friday—games preceded afternoon lessons in order to make use of the limited light available for outdoor pursuits at that time of year. Instead of heading out on to the games field from a quarter to four, as was the practice in the summer timetable, students were returning from their games afternoon at that time and preparing for two further lessons, concluding at six o'clock. Unsurprisingly the Civil War topic, which fell on Wednesday at the end of the day, was slow to catch fire. The heaviness would be the pattern until Easter and staff and pupils alike were struggling to adjust.

It seemed that Bear was more irritable than usual. He knew he had other factors on his mind unrelated to school and work was providing little relief. He even found himself in a rare argument with the genial Peter Walton, who suggested a late change in the teaching schedule for Year 11.

'I've just found out about this fantabulously great exhibition on Roosevelt's New Deal in London at the end of the month,' Peter enthused over lunch, his green-and-white striped bow tie seeming to endorse his scheme. 'Why don't all three of our groups start on the New Deal in a couple of weeks and push Stalin back till after Christmas? I'm sure old Joe wouldn't mind,' he added with a grin.

'He's hardly in a position to protest,' responded Bear in reference to the late Soviet dictator. 'Are you planning to take a trip there?'

'If the Head agrees, of course. But it's a good week to ask, don't you think? What a golden oppo to raise the department profile with the Head Man! And it makes much more sense to have gone to the exhibition after they have at least started on the topic. Take a look at this,' he said, reaching into his inside jacket pocket to produce a letter headed by a schools' historical society, of which he was a member. Scanning its contents, Bear realised it was an invitation to visit an exhibition at a London museum with a tailor-made guided visit for school parties including an interactive presentation on 'Roosevelt's New Deal: The Making of Modern America.'

Bear frowned, more than a little annoyed that the carefully agreed schedule of teaching could be tampered with at late notice. He knew what Peter meant by a good week, of course. The ISIC report on the recent inspection had just been published, with the school being awarded an overall 'Outstanding' category for teaching and 'Very Good' (with certain reservations on administrative procedures) for management. The Head had asked all staff to keep early Friday evening in their diaries free when a celebratory supper courtesy of the governors was planned.

Stephen Rawlinson was sure to be in a good mood for any slightly unorthodox requests. Bear was annoyed at Peter's proposal, as he had planned to develop the theme of dictatorship by moving seamlessly from Mao to Stalin and did not wish to break up the sequence. However, it was hard to resist Peter's logic on the need to be flexible and strike while the iron was hot.

'Have you spoken to Michael?' Bear asked, knowing already what Peter would say. The head of department, who taught the third history group for Year 11, would have to agree to the change of programmes for all three groups for the amendment to go ahead.

'Not yet,' Peter replied predictably. 'I thought if the two of us were agreed, he would be more likely to be flexible.'

'When do you hope to visit this exhibition?'

'Last week in November, just before the school exams. If I can speak to Michael and the Head today, or tomorrow at the latest, we have a chance of getting a guided visit booked, and then… game on!'

Reluctantly and somewhat grumpily, Bear gave way after protestation about disruption of schedule. Secretly, he hoped either Michael Streatham or the Head would veto the proposal on the grounds of short notice. Bear liked to plan things well in advance, although he had to concede that sometimes opportunism was called for. If Peter's visit got the go-ahead and Michael agreed to amend the Year 11 schedule, Bear would have to fortify his somewhat threadbare notes on 'United States between the Wars' that he had hoped to spend time on over the Christmas break. He had expected, as had been planned at a department meeting back in the summer to run through the dictators from Hitler to Stalin via Mussolini, Franco and Mao in a seamless sequence throughout the autumn and leave democracy to the new year. Democracy, it seemed, would not be dictated to. Having to react to changing circumstances, however, was not Bear's forte. In fact, he was seen very much more as a stabilising force at Princewood, especially on the games field, where he had more than once tempered Mac's overambitious and unrealistic tactics with more rudimentary, practical suggestions on how to win rugby games, which, when successfully implemented, earned Mac more than his share of the plaudits as the senior partner.

On returning to his flat that evening Bear noticed the bright red numeral announcing itself from his answer phone, indicating that one message had been received. He was disinclined to engage in any lengthy telephone conversation after the draining day he had experienced and was relieved that the caller had not been able to find him at home. He half-decided that making himself some supper should have priority over finding out what had been communicated, but thought better of it, just in case an emergency had arisen. He pressed 'play messages' and was surprised and curiously soothed to hear Sophie's voice, a very pleasing antidote to the day's stresses. His smile was short-lived, however, as she revealed the content of her message and a look of concern furrowed his brow. He played back the message a second time to digest what he had heard, then dialled her number.

Chapter Twelve
Travel Plans

As she gazed out over the flatlands of Essex amid the welcome late autumn sunshine, Sophie was unable to dispel the disquiet that had pursued her for much of the week. During the forty-minute journey out of London Liverpool Street, she had been able to calm her agitation, although pacified by the fact that most train travellers were heading in the opposite direction that Saturday morning, towards the capital. Her carriage was, therefore, barely a third full, enabling her to have time and space for own thoughts, undisturbed by noise or company. Her dominant thought was asking herself whether she was wasting her time making this journey at all. At least, she reflected, she would know the answer to that question by the end of the day.

Her mind turned once more to the telephone conversation she had had a few nights previously. She was relieved that Bear had returned her call and listened to her anxious relaying of the news she had read in the newspaper report that morning. She replayed in her mind the conversation and could not decide whether she was worrying herself unnecessarily, or right to share her concerns.

'It's the same area of Portugal, more or less,' she had emphasised, 'the same trade in jewellery, and he seemed pretty desperate to make a purchase last weekend.'

'But he wasn't trying to sell anything,' Bear had

responded without full conviction. 'He was just trying to buy your brooch on the cheap. Why should he be mixed up with this D'Oliveira chap? If he were, I would expect him to be lying low for a while.'

'What if he was planning to sell on the brooch and make a killing? If he knew D'Oliveira was close to being caught, he had limited time to cash in before the window of opportunity closed and anyone interested in buying got suspicious... And how do I know if I haven't bought stolen goods in the first place?'

Sophie had realised that some of her fears were less than rational, but they agreed that there was a possibility that Pedro was involved in some form of organised crime. They had no proof, however, and on the surface the Portuguese had simply presented as someone keen, perhaps a shade persistent, to make a purchase. Bear sensed that he was struggling to give any coherent advice over the phone and suggested they might meet up to discuss the newspaper report. He would scour the papers over the next couple of days to identify any further evidence either eliminating Pedro Gomes from suspicion of criminal activity or possibly implicating him therein.

'You're not free this Saturday, by any chance?' Sophie asked hopefully. She had worked out that Bear had some kind of church involvement and tended to keep Sundays free from other commitments. That suited her, as she often headed out of town on Sundays to a riding stables where she had a special arrangement to ride one or two of the horses that were more accommodating with visitors. So she naturally asked if he was free the following Saturday. She was surprised to hear that he was; his 'B' fifteen were idle that Saturday and he could meet and discuss any press findings that might relate to Pedro and any link with D'Oliveira.

'Can we meet up somewhere halfway? I don't want to drag you into London again. It's probably a false alarm, and I'm sorry if I'm wasting your time…'

Bear had assured her that he felt there were issues to sort out concerning the brooch and, in any case, he already felt involved. One way or another, they needed to talk things through.

Sophie had felt reassured by his support, although her anxiety remained as the train drew into Chelmsford station, where she alighted. She descended the steps to street level to leave the station. Having given him the scheduled arrival time of her train, she expected Bear to be punctual, from her experience of meeting him the previous Saturday. She was not disappointed. As she exited the station concourse, a familiar figure was waiting eagerly outside. His attire, on this occasion, was more casual than a week ago. Bear was wearing a dark green raincoat, faded blue jeans and dark trainers. Hardly a fashion statement, she thought, and slightly at odds with his rigour in sticking to schedules.

It had been a fraught few days for Bear. He had realised on Wednesday evening that Sophie needed help in making sense of the revelation about jewellery fraud and this Saturday was the only opportunity for a while for a face-to-face conversation. He was glad to be free of coaching duties that day, as this was his last free Saturday for a few weeks. On Thursday he had made a beeline for the school library and extracted the previous day's *Daily Telegraph* to ascertain whether that newspaper also carried details of the D'Oliveira story. It did, although Bear was not sure if the article that he managed to locate shed any further light on the developments

Sophie had reported to him the night before. He had helped himself to the otherwise unwanted newspaper, and later that day while in a launderette, picked up a discarded tabloid which also contained information on the arrest. On Friday he had learned to his dismay that Peter Walton's request for the exhibition visit had been granted, which meant a reorganisation in his Year 11 teaching schedule. The museum had been rung up and a school visit had been provisionally booked pending written confirmation, which Peter had duly posted that day. At least one school minibus was available that day and America had supplanted Russia in the timetable. Bear loved certainties and having to be flexible at short notice did not come easily to him.

He was, by his own admission, in something of a mood throughout Friday. The Head's celebratory drinks and buffet food party that evening could not have been a more relaxed affair. There was much light-hearted banter with conversation about amusing incidents in the inspection and many of his colleagues were in fine form. Yet even Alan Cartwright's attempt at joviality failed to lighten Bear's demeanour.

'Did I say that Franz and Martina send their greetings and were asking after you?' asked the linguist, referring to teachers from Fürstenwald, from which he had returned at half-term after a successful exchange trip.

'Yes, you did, Alan,' answered Bear, wondering if the wine was going to his colleague's head. As spouses were invited to this celebration, Alan's wife Wendy had agreed to drive, allowing her husband to indulge more freely.

'Oh, did I? They still remember that incident last year when you got those pupils lost in the middle of Nuremberg,' Alan chuckled to himself. At least, Bear noted, there would be no coherent refereeing observations that evening. He generated a forced smile at the recollection and resigned himself to staying an hour or so before making his excuses. He was pleased to slip away largely unnoticed.

'Hello,' Bear greeted Sophie, relieved to dismiss school matters from his mind for a few hours, at least.

'We meet again,' he added, already recognising that this prepared line was becoming a bit wooden.

'Thank you so much for agreeing to meet,' she replied, 'I really don't know what to do.'

'Well, as I said the other day, the best thing is to have a good look at these articles first, and then see if we need to do anything. Where can we get a nice quiet cup of something?' This was a question to himself as much as to Sophie, as he assumed Chelmsford was new territory for both of them.

'I don't know about "quiet", but I do know a nice café not far from here.'

'You know Chelmsford, then?'

'I was here about a month ago when I was covering East Anglia. We stopped in the Café Moulin for an hour between school visits. It's got a very nice atmosphere, but I don't suppose it will be quiet at this time on a Saturday morning.' It had just gone a quarter to eleven and the streets were busy with weekend shoppers.

'That may be no bad thing,' Bear replied. 'It's probably better to discuss such matters in an atmosphere where everyone is wrapped up in their own conversations than when there's a deathly hush and we have to keep our voices right down.'

'This is starting to feel a bit like James Bond, don't you think?' wondered Sophie, 'I'm not sure this subterfuge is my cup of tea.'

'Talking of which… lead on to the Moulin…'

They passed through the covered shopping centre on to one of the side streets and entered the Café Moulin. As predicted, it was fairly full, with several tables already occupied, but they were able to find a table recently vacated near the window. The French theme was apparent with checked red-and-white tablecloths and accordion music being played in the background. All the staff wore berets, which Bear thought just a little over the top. They seated themselves at right angles to each other. A waitress took their order. Bear ordered a café crème and Sophie a herbal tea. As they waited, Sophie mentioned that Emily had had the bright idea to spend a pleasant hour or so in the café before commitments later in the day.

'Our Essex girl was a mine of local information,' Sophie added, smiling, but then realised that the time for small talk was later, and she opened her shoulder bag and withdrew an envelope, cautiously looking around her to check that no one was watching. No one was; they were all engrossed in their chat. She pulled out the photocopied article and showed it to Bear. He read it carefully before passing on his initial assessment, forming a mental picture of the apparent geographical scope of D'Oliveira's operations:

A police spokesman expressed contentment that the person considered to be responsible for extorting hundreds of people of vast sums of money had been arrested, but there was no room for complacency. There was a strong possibility, he warned, that stolen or undervalued items were being sold across a network of outlets in the Minho, Trás-os-Montes and Beira Alta regions. In such cases the public was advised to

147

contact the local police…

'So what has this D'Oliveira done exactly?' Bear asked as much to himself as to Sophie. At that moment, the waitress returned with their drinks. Sophie waited until privacy was restored before replying.

'Conned people into having jewellery valued, then giving the customer a gross over-valuation. He gets one of his agents to put in an offer well under its true value, but much more than the customer expected. The customer thinks, shame, I thought it would go for more, but better than what I originally thought. Meanwhile, the agent, usually via a go-between, has bought the item and sold it on at a much higher price, often using pseudo-knowledge of antiques to justify its value.'

Bear raised an eyebrow, impressed at Sophie's explanation. 'You've certainly done your research. But a lot of this stuff gets sold at auctions. Surely there would be some experts to smell a rat, or simply correct the estimates that are given?'

'That's just the thing, though. Some of the auctioneers are in on it. Once the items are sold, they either mysteriously mislay or alter any records of the estimated price and simply put the sale down to overenthusiastic bidding. And D'Oliveira had his own people in the auction rooms just to pump up the bidding artificially.'

Bear smiled at the recollection of the jovial Hugo Chisholm. He couldn't imagine him being involved in such skulduggery, but you never can tell. He then remembered a line in the tabloid that referred to 'infiltration of auctioneers and other outlets' in northern Portugal. It was beginning to make sense.

'But why should our friend Pedro be involved?' Bear

wondered. 'I mean, all he was doing last week was to buy an item he thought he could sell on at a profit, like anyone else. You said no thanks. End of story.'

'I just don't know,' Sophie replied, unable to rid herself of the unease at the memory of the attempted purchase of her brooch. 'It's just that we're talking about his patch, and he clearly travels abroad, so if he is mixed up with D'Oliveira he would be someone to use to sell on the items at a decent profit without leaving too much of a trail. Of course, Pedro may be completely innocent, for all we know.'

'I'm not sure it's any of our business, though,' Bear said unconvincingly. 'However...,' he paused, uncertain how he should continue this line of conversation, but realising he had to proceed, 'we're still left with the question of the true value of your brooch.' He felt he was being a touch impudent in using the plural pronoun 'we', but Sophie gave no sign of taking offence. In fact, she seemed to welcome his concern and involvement.

Sophie took a sip of her herbal tea and gazed thoughtfully out of the window for a moment, weighing her options. The pause felt much longer than it was. Finally, she said,

'I suppose I must get it valued properly. I can't just hang on to it with a vague idea of its worth. I need to know one way or the other.'

'I'm sorry I've dragged you into this,' Bear replied sympathetically. 'If I hadn't gone to the auctioneers in Norwich, you'd be none the wiser. It was not my business to go investigating.'

'No, I'm glad you did. I'd like to think I would have checked its value one day... but probably not till I have grandchildren and want to leave them something.'

They both hesitated, neither daring to voice what they knew should be the course of action. Eventually Bear broke the silence.

'I suppose we could go to Lisbon and find out. Any expert would surely be based in the capital. In this country I expect all we'll get are vague estimates.' As Sophie did not respond immediately, he added, 'We might be able to track Pedro down if he's at home.'

As he said this, memories of Bonhoeffer returning to Germany to potential danger and Jonah being given a second chance to preach to the feared Ninevites came to mind. He wondered whether he was being given a nudge to go back to Portugal, not as a tourist this time, but to fulfil a specific mission. He was about to dismiss this thought as absurd and a product of a hyperactive imagination when Sophie's reply took him by surprise.

'Perhaps, but it's quite a hike to the Beira Alta from Lisbon, about four or five hours. That would take out most of a day just getting there.'

'You've worked out where he lives?' Bear asked, surprised that Sophie had taken the trouble to find out the location of Pedro Gomes' home town, but also slightly disappointed that he could no longer demonstrate any superior knowledge. He had kept Pedro's business card, on which the dealer's town and phone number were printed. As it looked as if Pedro worked for himself, Bear guessed that the number was for his residence.

'I did do a geography degree, you know,' Sophie said in mock admonishment at Bear's apparently low expectations of her powers of research, 'and I did keep his card. I don't know why; it just felt like it might come in useful.'

While she was speaking, Bear's mind was assailed with possible plans for a relaxing first week of the Christmas holidays. After all, that was the advantage of being a teacher, especially in the independent system where you got longer holidays. Work like mad for weeks on end preparing lessons, marking books, performing duties, fulfilling pastoral responsibilities, writing reports, attending parents' evenings, coaching sports teams with numerous fixtures to attend or referee—then crash out exhausted at the end of term, especially the longer autumn term and enjoy a leisurely week to get ready for Christmas. Get Christmas shopping done in the middle of that week while the shops were relatively quiet, rehearsal on the Thursday evening for Cynthia Standish's nativity production that he had foolishly agreed to be a part of, the tennis club Christmas dinner and disco on the Friday night, for which he had yet to send a response. All could be taken at a leisurely pace. But whether it was a little voice inside his head or just a solid tug on his conscience, Bear knew that he would need to be elsewhere for that week, depending on Sophie's answer to his next question.

'I know this sounds crazy, but...' he paused before continuing with more resolution than he expected, 'how would you feel about going back to Portugal? We could consult a jewellery expert, probably in Lisbon, and possibly even call in on Pedro if it seems right.'

'Go back to Portugal?' she asked. 'When were you thinking of?'

'Well, how about the third week in December? I'm sure we could find a couple of rooms for a few nights at this time of year if needed.' He was relieved to insert 'a couple' seamlessly into his suggestion and hoped it had come across as such, just in case his idea was misinterpreted.

'Well, I don't know…' Sophie was in reflective mood. 'I suppose…'

'I break up on the Friday before. I don't have any particular commitments until the following Saturday. If we need a few days, we could look up Pedro. I don't know if there's any chance of you getting time off…'

Sophie had averted her eyes momentarily to gaze out to the street outside, but now returned her attention fully to her companion. 'We're never that busy in the week before Christmas. Schools don't really want visits then, they're too busy winding down. It's mainly just admin and sales reports then and sometimes preparing for the odd book launch. I'm sure I can get leave for that week. Anyway, I'm owed a favour from my boss.' She recalled Max's exact words when she finished her three weeks' substitution for Ryan, 'Cheers, Soph, I owe you one.'

'So shall we go to Lisbon that week and sort out this business once and for all?' Bear asked.

Sophie paused before saying, 'Let's do it. If you're sure you don't mind helping.'

Bear replied that he wouldn't forgive himself if he didn't make every effort to bring the matter to a conclusion. Sophie raised questions about the practicalities, such as tracking down the appropriate experts. No problem, said Bear. He happened to know that Michael Streatham had a contact at the British Museum who was privy to a whole list of international specialists in historical artefacts. If he could persuade Michael to release his friend's number, he might be able to contact the appropriate Portuguese expert and even arrange a consultation for the first week of the Christmas holidays. For a teacher, that was the window of opportunity. Bear had spent his career fielding good-natured complaints from friends in other fields about his long holidays, but he did not have the liberty of being flexible with his leave. Anything significant or time-consuming that needed to be done had to be left to the holidays. He had to strike when the iron was hot; that could not be until mid-December, but he had to seize the opportunity with both hands when it came. Talking of striking while the iron was hot….

'Do you see what I see?' he asked, gesturing to Sophie at the street outside.

'The street,' she answered, puzzled, 'and a few shoppers.'

'The other side of the street. Big yellow sign?'

Sophie noticed immediately and looked back at Bear as if to ascertain that he was serious. It was clear that he was. It was an unspoken agreement that they should drink up and head across the street. Bear finished his by now cold café crème. Sophie insisted on paying the bill and they exited the Café Moulin. Twenty minutes later they took their leave of another premises, having honoured Granger's Travel Agents with their custom and secured two return flight tickets to Lisbon for the third Monday in December, returning the following Friday. They stayed in Chelmsford for lunch, during which possible scenarios and tactics for their stay were provisionally discussed. When they parted later that afternoon, they were both conscious that the third week in December promised to be a very full and demanding one. Bear's thoughts turned to what was likely to be an even busier November than usual and how he would make an unusual request to Michael Streatham on Monday morning.

Chapter Thirteen
Agent Bear

'Sir! Sir! Mister Hoskins!'

Bear was about to re-enter the staff room at a quarter past eight on the following Monday morning, having exited briefly to photocopy an article he deemed useful for discussion of Civil War topics with the sixth form. He turned to see two excited girls from 7P eager to impart information to him.

'Can I help you, ladies?' he asked theatrically.

'Sir, sir, we've got it!' the shorter, blonde partner enthusiastically declared. Her friend, more solidly built and dark haired, was clearly the supporting member of this team, and just nodded keenly in confirmation.

'You've got what, Hannah?' Bear queried, feigning ignorance, although he knew full well what she was talking about.

'The thing about Jonah, the sign of Jonah. You know, the thing you asked us to find out last lesson.'

Although not in the least taken aback that this was the issue the girls wished to raise, given the fact that they were in 7P and RS was his only involvement with the class, he was agreeably surprised that the voluntary task he had set should have received a response some five days after the lesson. Usually it was overnight or not at all. Any later than that and the eleven-year-old mind was consumed with countless other issues of the day. Not so this time; it transpired later that the two girls had met over the weekend and conversation had turned to school matters. Hence the girls' decision to find out the answer to the question, by means of a little-used family Bible.

'And is this a joint decision? Have you both come to the same answer?'

'We found out together,' replied Hannah.

'I see,' answered Bear in non-committal fashion.

'You didn't say we couldn't,' the other girl asserted, finally joining in the conversation.

'Quite correct, Lucy. So what have you found out?'

'Well, Jesus said…' Hannah began, swiftly producing a Bible from behind her back and opening to a bookmarked page in Matthew's gospel. She located the passage with her finger and read it out to the teacher. '"A wicked and adulterous generation asks for a sign! But none will be given it except the sign of the prophet Jonah. For as Jonah was three days and three nights in the belly of a huge fish, so the Son of Man will be three days and three nights in the heart of the earth."'

'Well done!' Bear smiled as he congratulated the two students on their research. 'You will need to get your school diaries, then. Let's just make a quick visit to my classroom before registration.'

The two girls beamed with pleasure. They knew that 'getting your school diaries' meant that the teacher concerned would insert a school stamp on a dedicated page in the individual pupil's diary and sign his or her name under the stamp to indicate who was issuing the reward and for what subject. That would constitute the promised house point for the successful student. Hannah had been confident of this outcome and said, 'We've already got them, sir.'

Bear opened his classroom, sat at his desk as he opened a drawer to extract the Princewood School House Point stamp, firmly pressed down on the stamp pad and transmitted the image to the required spot in each of the girls' diaries with the firm flourish of a border customs official declaring authorisation of passage into his country. He pretended to forget and just remember in the nick of time the other part of the bargain, producing a bag full of mini-chocolate bars, from which each pupil gratefully selected one. The girls thanked Bear and turned to leave when he asked them,

'And what does it mean about the Son of Man being in the heart of the earth for three days and three nights?'

Hannah looked puzzled at Bear, then at her companion, suddenly apparently anxious that the reward could be rescinded unless this sudden hurdle were overcome. This time, however, it was her friend who spoke up.

'It's all about Jesus dying and coming back from the dead,' said Lucy, as though she was stating the obvious and bemused that the teacher could be asking such a simple question.

Interesting, thought Bear, this was someone with no church background at all, unlikely to have any advantage in answering this particular question, but one who quietly took things in and weighed them up carefully. One to watch for the future, he noted.

* * * *

Much as Bear liked Vivaldi, hearing the repeated strains of the *Four Seasons* was testing his patience that Tuesday morning.

He had dialled the number at the British Museum and been told that he was being held in a queue. In between the sublime music of the famous Italian composer, he was regularly reminded how his call was important to them and that they, presumably some human beings working at that illustrious institution, would answer his call as soon as possible. Bear resigned himself to a lengthy wait as the staff room emptied towards the end of break. His one free period that day was likely to be eaten into considerably by the time he got through.

It had been a frustrating twenty-four hours. It had begun well with the unexpected enthusiasm of Hannah and Lucy brightening up the start of the week with their answer to his teaser. That was one thing that always motivated him about teaching. Children were so unpredictable and often lifted your spirits at an unexpected moment, as occasionally, did colleagues. A drab mid-term day was more than once illuminated by a cheerful remark or pleasantry and even the darkest times did not stay dark too long. However, later that morning he had the business of approaching Michael Streatham in their common free period and asking for the name and phone number of his friend who worked for the British Museum and could probably supply the name of the appropriate expert in a particular field of exhibits. Bear was relieved that their conversation did not extend throughout the lesson, but Michael did not have his friend's number to hand and promised to bring it to work the next day. When Bear arrived at school on Tuesday, Michael's immediate expression indicated that he had forgotten to do so. Michael suggested contacting the museum in working hours, giving his friend's name, Brian Worthington. Rather than wait another day for Brian's home number to be provided, Bear decided to bite the bullet and attempt to contact him at work. That means of communication was proving to be easier said than done.

The telephone was located at the quiet end of the long staff room furthest from the hot-drinks dispensers. Bear had aimed to begin his conversation five minutes before the end of break when the room was fairly full but knew that he was sufficiently far from most of the occupants of the room to conduct his conversation in relative peace and hear what was being said by the person at the other end of the line. After break finished the staff room would be virtually empty and he would have no difficulty hearing. He was vaguely aware of a couple of colleagues poring over a document before one of them got up and left, leaving the other to reflect further on the contents. Still the dulcet tones of Vivaldi played as he was reminded how important his call was to the British Museum. Finally, after some ten minutes hanging on the line, he was connected.

'Brian Worthington speaking.'

'Hello, Mr Worthington, my name's Hoskins. I'm a friend of Michael Streatham at Princewood School in Suffolk.' Bear avoided disclosing his first name, not out of respect for formalities, but simply to avoid drawing attention to it and being obliged to supply unnecessary explanations. He need not have worried.

'Oh yes, Bear Hoskins. Michael said you might call. How can I help?'

As Bear began his explanation, armed with notes that he had gleaned from Hugo Chisholm about the brooch's provenance and his recollection of its design, he was aware that the staff room was now virtually empty. Kitchen staff were starting to clear away coffee mugs and wipe down tables, and just a few teachers were lingering who were not teaching immediately after break. Bear became increasingly conscious that from now on anything he said would inevitably be heard by anyone present and no matter how hard he tried to make the conversation sound as matter-of-fact and mundane, he could hardly blame anyone for being intrigued at what was audible at Bear's end of the line.

'I know this is an unusual request, but... I gather you have some useful contacts abroad... Portugal, jewellery and metal ware... Yes, 17th, possibly 18th century... I understand thousands, at least, if genuine... Who's our man in Lisbon...? Could I arrange to meet him...? How could I make contact...? It's on behalf of a friend... No one knows apart from ourselves...'

It was with a marked sinking feeling that Bear groaned inwardly as he realised that the solitary occupant of the nearest coffee table was none other than John Billington. The Head of Physics had been discussing some document relating to changes to the GCSE science syllabus and after the colleague had departed, he had picked up the staff room copy of the *Daily Telegraph* for a quick five-minutes' scan of the day's news before returning to his classroom. The five minutes grew longer as Bear's telephone conversation became audible. Oh no, not Billers! sighed Bear quietly. Of all his colleagues, with the possible exception of Claudine, the one person he would least like to overhear his half of the dialogue with the British Museum employee was John Billington. Not that Billers was indiscreet; he would certainly not divulge the details of a private conversation to any children. He would, however, have difficulty in not passing on a tasty morsel of high drama with other teachers. That was Billers: larger than life, gregarious, delighting in the pantomime that was the daily twists and turns of the teaching profession. He meant no harm, Bear knew; he just could not be relied upon to keep his mouth shut. But why couldn't everyone be like Linda Porter, quiet and unassuming, economical with her words, making sure that everything she said was positive, affirmative and supportive? As she had demonstrated earlier that morning, for instance, in telling Bear how Lucy and Hannah were thrilled to receive their house points and that it sounded like an ingenious conundrum Bear had set her tutees. With Billers, however, Bear knew that some further awkward explanations on a par with his repeated denials of intimacy with Sophie at The Anchor earlier in the term were now inevitable. The resumption of the exchange with Brian Worthington after the museum official had paused to consult his files will have done little to dampen John Billington's curiosity.

'Yes, I have a pen… Go ahead… Sixty, six zero…? I've got that, thank you… Mark "confidential"…? Around the 14th of next month … I won't be able to get away until then … Once we land in Lisbon, time will be of the essence… I'll only be in Portugal for a short time and need to make it count… Thank you, Mr Worthington, you've been very helpful… I hope so too… Goodbye.'

Bear replaced the receiver and stood silent for a few seconds, taking in the details he had noted down and starting to contemplate his next move. He had no time to develop such contemplation as John Billington emerged from behind the pretended seclusion of the newspaper.

'Well, you are a dark horse, Bear, if I may say so. Couldn't help overhearing a lot of that. I didn't know we had a super sleuth in our midst. Or should I say secret agent? Sounds really exciting. "Our man in Lisbon" sounds a shady character. Hope you make contact with him all right.'

'Yes, thank you, John. So do I,' Bear replied, trying to be as restrained as possible in making it clear that these were not details for public consumption.

'So you have "just a short time to make it count"?' Billers probed further. 'I wonder what "it" might be?'

Bear was not playing ball. 'Let's just say it's a long story,' he said, turning to leave the room.

'Oh don't worry, Bear, your secret's safe with me. Mum's the word,' Billers chuckled, tapping his nose with his index finger in a gesture of collusion.

That evening, Bear reflected on the absurdity of trying to keep secret his planned second visit to Portugal that year. He had nothing to hide, after all. He was going to Lisbon to consult an expert on the value of an item of jewellery. Yes, that was his plan, and that was what he would say when asked about his plans for the Christmas holiday. Perfectly normal question, perfect normal response. Alone? No, he was going with a friend. Male or female? Female. So is it her jewellery then? Well, yes, as a matter of fact it is. She asked me to join her. No, that's not quite accurate—we agreed that both of us should go. No, this isn't sounding convincing or credible. So how long are you going for? About four or five days. So you're planning to see the sights of Lisbon? Possibly. We may be going out of the city for a while to see somebody. A friend. A mutual friend, sort of. Perfectly normal thing to do in midwinter. Hang on a moment, didn't you say something about returning a brooch to a saleswoman back in September? My, you are a dark horse, Bear. Have a lovely time! Oh, forget it, Bear said to himself, I'll just say I'm going to Lisbon with a friend, and people can draw whatever conclusions they want.

* * * *

That same evening, secrecy was also uppermost in the minds of the residents of a comfortable looking but unspectacular suburban dwelling in the Beira Alta region of eastern Portugal. Having entertained his uninvited guests for some thirty minutes in his study, Pedro Gomes escorted the police inspector and his sergeant from the premises. For the second time in as many weeks, he had been visited for 'a chat'. More like a grilling, he thought. If that was a friendly enquiry, what would a 'chat' down at the station be like? He had felt distinctly uncomfortable throughout the meeting, and by no means sure that his answers had assured the police of his innocence.

'I hope you catch them, whoever these accomplices are,' Pedro said as the officers departed.

'Oh, don't worry, sir, we will,' the inspector replied, 'we have our eyes everywhere. You'd be surprised.'

As he closed the door behind them, Pedro stared ahead, deep in thought. His mind performed somersaults as he recalled the various places that he had visited over the past two months. The police had 'eyes everywhere', including abroad. Interpol was involved in the case. Surely not as far as London? The woman with the brooch seemed to know the far north of Portugal quite well. The area was hardly top of the tourist destinations list. Why was she there? Part of some complex sting operation? Or if she had never visited the region, maybe she had just memorised an elaborate cover story. No, Pedro, calm down, she was just a lady wearing a brooch... who happened to be familiar with an obscure border town. At that moment, his wife Luisa emerged from the lounge to question him further and cut short his anxious recollections.

'What did they want this time?' she asked, not unreasonably. 'More about D'Oliveira?'

'More about his associates this time. They showed me photos of several men they suspect of being involved. I thought I recognised one or two from auctions, but I couldn't be sure. I wasn't much help.'

'And that took up half an hour?'

'They were very thorough. Spent most of the time reminding me that any detail I could think of could be critical. I kept telling them I'd never met D'Oliveira, but I don't think they're convinced. They'll still be watching me.'

Both Pedro and Luisa agreed to maintain secrecy concerning the recent police visits.

That, for the moment, was relatively easy, as Pedro could point to numerous business contacts. Discussions out of working hours were not unheard of and neighbours were unlikely to ask awkward questions. Luisa asked Pedro whether he might have inadvertently said something to someone to attract suspicion, but he didn't think so. That was not strictly true. He had almost certainly said too much on his last visit to London. But how could he have remained silent that day at the market? He had been fortunate enough to have had a good look at the woman's brooch, and he was almost certain of its provenance. He could hardly not make a bid for it.

Maybe following them to a pub had not been the best idea, but he had reasoned that a relaxed chat sitting down over a few beers might change their minds. He had handled the situation poorly, he recalled ruefully. If he could only make contact with the couple again, maybe he could exercise his powers of persuasion more effectively. What were their names again? The woman was called Sophie or Sophia, he was certain of that. He had a vague recollection that the man was called Ben, but he wasn't sure. Perhaps they lived near the market should he return to London soon? Clutching at straws. Face it, Pedro, he said to himself, you had your chance and blew it, and that's the end of the matter. Yet he knew in his heart that it could not be.

Chapter Fourteen
Excuses, excuses

Such was his state of high excitement, mixed with apprehension, bewilderment and a wariness of the unknown that Bear found himself formulating a fresh Plan B for almost every day of the month between his phone conversation with Brian Worthington and his departure for Portugal.

He was constantly considering a perplexing set of alternatives for how to proceed. What if the recommended expert turned out to be unavailable that week? Or only available at the end, leaving insufficient time to pay a call on Pedro Gomes? Should he and Sophie try to track down another expert? What if Pedro wasn't at home? What if he were mixed up with D'Oliveira? What if Sophie and Bear going to visit Pedro put them in danger? How should they react under such circumstances? By the end of November Bear had had enough of the jungle of 'what ifs' and hypothetical plans that he decided, much against his nature that was always to plan and prepare thoroughly, to 'go with the flow'.

The first current to surge downstream was extremely positive news. Within a week of writing to the expert at the Instituto de Cultura Nacional in Lisbon, he received a reply, in immaculate English, confirming that Senhor Manuel Cardoso was able to meet Mr Hoskins and Miss Bingham on the Tuesday of that week at 9.30 a.m. Bear had felt slightly embarrassed at writing a long explanation of his request in English and apologised for his lack of Portuguese, but Senhor Cardoso was apparently used to fielding such enquiries from the Anglosphere. Bear had excitedly written back the same day, offering profuse thanks and letting Sophie know that phase one of their project was set to go. All being well, they would have sufficient time to head out of the Portuguese capital that week and pay the antiques dealer a visit, if required.

The last fortnight of term was characterised by a series of apologies and explanations.

Bear felt compelled to apologise to Peter Walton for his grumpiness in being reluctant to support the altered Year 11 timetable. Unexpectedly, the museum visit had been not only a success but very well subscribed. So much so that two minibuses were required for the trip. Initially, Peter had planned on being accompanied just by the obligatory female member of staff (in the absence of a historian, Rachel Rhodes had agreed to fill that role). However, as parental consent forms were quickly returned, indicating that some twenty-six history students wished to find out more about The Making of Modern America, it became clear that a further minibus driver was needed. Bear ended up driving the second vehicle, accompanied by Katie, the New Zealander gap-year student. The interactive aspect of the visit certainly kept the students absorbed and Bear was forced to acknowledge that Peter, for all his superficial flamboyance, had a good eye for a genuinely valuable educational opportunity. The pupils were buzzing in the days after the trip and much-needed impetus was given to the course before the inevitable return to the dictators, now rescheduled for January. Be flexible, Bear told himself, don't put yourself in a straitjacket that prevents you seeing what can be achieved by doing things a bit differently.

Apology number two had to be delivered to Cynthia Standish in early December. Bear had agreed to take part in Cynthia's nativity production on the Sunday before Christmas, regretting slightly the impulsive decision in inspection week to attend a preparatory meeting that lured him into accepting an acting role. It was decided that five formal rehearsals on successive Thursday evenings would be needed to prepare the cast to a reasonable standard, followed by a dress rehearsal on the Saturday afternoon, the eve of the performance. Knowing that Cynthia was likely to be too busy directing to receive his apology for absence for the session in two weeks' time, Bear decided to appear at the church hall ten minutes early to ensure that his explanation was received and understood. The cryptic statement that he was unexpectedly needing to be away for most of that week but would be back in time for the dress rehearsal, was taken in good-humoured, if somewhat theatrical manner.

'O Melchior, Melchior! Wherefore art thou, Melchior?' complained the minister's wife. 'What am I going to do with you, Melchior? I've got Herod away next Thursday and I was hoping to have a good go over you three kings meeting Herod in two weeks' time... Right, it'll have to be tonight, can't leave everything till the dress rehearsal. We will major on the scene where you three pay your respects to Herod and you all feel uncomfortable that he's up to no good and is a bit too eager to learn about another king being born in Bethlehem. Anyway, I thought you had broken up that week. Didn't know you were going away?' The last remark carried a definite rising intonation in Cynthia's voice, and Bear sensed he needed to offer a more precise explanation for his anticipated absence.

'I wasn't, but something came up that means… I have to be away for a few days,' he said, unconvincingly, 'but I will definitely be back in time for Saturday.'

Fortunately, the church hall was beginning to fill as other would-be thespians entered the building. Mary Brewer, assigned to play a shepherdess, but normally to be found as a bank cashier during working hours, greeted them both and immediately engaged Cynthia in conversation about church services in Advent, much to Bear's relief. He would not have to go through another delicate explanation where he wanted to be honest but simultaneously preferred to prevent any details about valuable jewellery, still less rumours about unexpected developments in his private life, being in the public domain. He was spared further reference to his future absence as the cast assembled, ready for the rehearsal to begin. In all, a dozen members of Grove Street Baptist Church had been recruited for this nativity play 'for the whole family', as Cynthia termed it. She had written the piece to blend in humour, bordering on pantomime, but retaining a serious message. Having read through the script, Bear acknowledged that she had struck a good balance, one that would attract visitors and communicate the appropriate seasonal emphases.

After Bear had observed several scenes involving other characters, he was summoned to the front of the hall with his fellow magi. John Compton, playing the role of Balthazar, worked as assistant manager of a supermarket in his day job, while Nigel Burrows, semi-retired, alias Gaspar, helped at a garden centre two days a week when not treading the boards. The three wise men were visiting Jerusalem, trying to receive guidance as to where the King of the Jews was to be born. The star they had followed had guided them thus far, but they needed to know precisely where their search would end. Cynthia had very precise instructions to deliver.

'Right, wise men, you are going to be a bit wary of Herod, but respectful. Remember he's receiving you as honoured foreign dignitaries, so you need to at least act as if you're taking him at his word. You know Herod's got a bit of a reputation for cruelty, but you set that to one side because you want to find out where this new king is to be born. Everyone ready, page 23, starting with Herod saying "Welcome". Off you go, Herod.'

'Welcome to Jerusalem, gentlemen,' Herod, played by Keith Steel, local businessman in his mid-fifties, said with a warm, condescending smile of a Dickensian bank manager while at the same time communicating respect with his words. 'I gather you have come a long way. If I can be of service to you in your mission, it would be an honour to assist.'

Before any of the wise men could respond, Stephanie Walker, a young mother in her late twenties, stepped forward to read her part. 'His Majesty welcomes you to Jerusalem, gentleman. He gathers you have come a long way and says if he can be of service to you... sorry,' Stephanie's face creased, and she gave way to a fit of giggles. 'Sorry, guys, I'll be all right in a minute.'

'Now, interpreter,' Cynthia wagged her finger in mock-admonishment, 'I know you're going to be made redundant in a moment, but you need to act as the king's most trusted servant. Try again from "His Majesty welcomes"...'

Stephanie delivered her speech, this time without cracking up at the farce Cynthia had instilled. The magi responded.

'Your Majesty is most gracious,' said Balthazar with a bow.

'Your Majesty is most gracious,' repeated Stephanie, turning to Herod, who responded with a nod and a smile.

'It is indeed an honour to be received in Your Majesty's courts,' said Gaspar.

'It is indeed an honour for them to be received in Your Majesty's courts,' echoed Stephanie, turning again to Herod.

'We have been privileged in our studies to have acquired a knowledge of the language of the Hebrews,' Bear, alias Melchior, added.

'They have been privileged in their studies to have acquired a knowledge of the language of the Hebrews.' Stephanie transmitted Bear's words, straining for her best automaton voice.

'I know that!' Herod replied in an exasperated tone. 'I understood that bit. I don't think I will be requiring your services this morning, interpreter.'

'His Majesty says he doesn't think he will be requiring my services... oops,' Stephanie began, before discreetly withdrawing off-stage.

'Excellent, interpreter!' Cynthia called after her. 'I love the military obedience in reporting everyone's words almost to the letter and the "oops" was brilliantly timed. If we can just sort out the giggles, we've got that bit nailed. Now after a pause, Herod asks you three what you're doing here. On you go, Herod.'

'So what brings you to Judea, gentlemen?' Keith Steel asked.

The wise men explained their quest, and were redirected by Herod, who had already ascertained their purpose, and was happy to point them on their way.

'My advisors tell me that the prophets confirm that the king is to be born in Bethlehem, the city of David, some twenty miles to the south.'

The magi played their part with feeling and communicated sufficient awe, reverence, wonder and not a little fear of Herod to satisfy the play's director. Cynthia had just a few concluding remarks to deliver before moving on to another scene.

'Don't forget, wise men, that whilst you are convinced that this mission is really important and you can't back down, you are aware that to many people it will look crazy, but it is something you must do. There may be danger ahead, but you have to go through with it. So look determined and serious, even in the funny bits.'

Bear had difficulty concentrating for the rest of the rehearsal. The director's guidance seemed to apply not just to the play, but to his plans for the first week of the holidays. Had Cynthia been speaking to someone about his forthcoming travels? He was grateful that for the remainder of the evening, he had no more lines to deliver. The rehearsal concluded amicably at nine o'clock sharp, and Bear returned to his flat to devote some time to the laborious challenge of end-of-term reports. Knowing his energy levels were likely to be limited at that stage of the evening, he selected his RS reports for 7P as his chosen group for the evening. Since he saw this class only once a week, there was nothing hugely distinctive to say about every pupil; he would outline what had been covered that term and give an indication of each child's level of participation in class and clarity of written work. For a few, such as Toby, whose observations showed an astuteness beyond his years, and Hannah and Lucy, with their enthusiasm in securing house points, he had more to say and could wax lyrical about their contributions.

Further apologies ensued over the last weeks of term. He had to explain to the organiser of the Tennis Club dinner dance that he would not be attending that year, after having faithfully participated for the past three years. Beryl Stanton expressed disappointment when she rang up to check that there was no mistake, and then asked whether it was much warmer in Lisbon at this time of year when Bear disclosed why he would be absent. When Mac casually asked whether Bear would be up for a visit to the Anchor one night that week, Bear decided there was no point in caution and said that he was spending a few days in Portugal with someone he met there in the summer. Yes, he confirmed, the sales rep from the booksellers. The raised eyebrows and almost complicit smile from Rob McAllister indicated that he felt he wanted to congratulate Bear on a romantic liaison, as if he were a gold prospector who had finally struck rich after months of fruitless digging. Fine, thought Bear, easier for him to think that than for me to talk about brooches and consulting experts. When Bear asked what Mac would be doing in the first days of the holiday, the lack of a committed answer suggested that, not for the first time, the English teacher's romantic aspirations had been disappointed.

* * * *

Meanwhile, back in north London, Sophie was doing her own share of apologising. She had informed the personnel department that she would be taking the week before

Christmas off as part of her allotted leave and left a memo in Max Chandler's in tray. She knew that her boss would be away for a fortnight helping set up the new office in Glasgow, recruiting the first two sales staff. Assuming that there would be few urgent demands on her time during the planned week of absence, she had little doubt that her request would be granted, especially as Max had categorically stated that he 'owed her one'. When she entered the Foundation Books building one morning in late November for an office-based day, largely dealing with filing and passing on records of sales from three schools visits in Sussex that week, she knocked on the half-open door to Max's office to confirm that he had received news of her request. His response, even by Max's theatrical standards, was warm, supportive and accommodating, as expected, but also conveying intense disappointment, the genuineness of which Sophie was at a loss to discern.

He had seen her memo on his return from Glasgow and had had time to formulate a response. 'Yeah, I got it, Soph. Thanks for telling me. Like I said, I owe you one for stepping in for Ry and getting Em on her feet back in September. So if you need time off, no probs. Got all bases covered. But you could have been just the person we need that week,' he paused with a heavy sigh.

'Oh really, Max?' asked Sophie, suspiciously. 'How's that?'

'London Christmas Book Fair. I need a couple of people to run a stand there. I thought of you straight away, and then... I saw your memo,' he added, almost wistfully.

Sophie cast a puzzled look at the sales manager. She was aware of the book fair, a relatively recent addition to the booksellers' calendar, which had been running for some five years now. The reason for her raised eyebrows was that the education department had hitherto not been involved in this event, which had mainly focused on fiction, biography and more popular genres. As she and her colleagues had more than once joked, receiving a new edition on the latest science syllabus or a fresh look at algebraic equations was unlikely to rank high on anyone's wish list of Christmas gifts. Consequently, the fair had been given a wide berth by the department. Not so this year. It was obvious to Sophie that this sudden change of policy would need explanation, and she waited for Max to elaborate. It seemed that he was extending his pause for maximum effect.

'I thought we didn't get involved in the fair,' she remarked. 'And why should you need me especially?'

Max had hoped Sophie would ask the inevitable question so that he could pay her the compliment that would be of value to him as a manager in the future. A shrewd investment, he thought to himself. He explained Foundation Books' participation that year.

'Little Mo has got a new book to launch. Sort of sequel to *Doing It My Way*. It's called *One Step Ahead*, with a glorious subtitle 'motivational management methods for a new millennium'. Catchy, eh? We reckon, and Susan Mortimer has checked this out as she's been to the fair every year, that there is a market for people wanting to know the right motivational psychology at all levels of management, in all fields. This one's not aimed at teachers this time, but anyone with a management responsibility. Teachers who read his first book would be interested in Mo's second book, though. It's about the psychology of persuasion.'

'So how would I have been any use?'

'We need someone with a good track record and who can vouch for how helpful Mo's first book has been. You certainly got the ball rolling with selling *Doing It My Way* while you were with Em, and since you've gone back to K and S your sales have rocketed. In fact, I can reveal that you are our top salesperson for October of that volume. You would have been just the person to present the book at the stand at the fair. Full steamo, or what?'

'Full steam ahead, indeed,' concurred Sophie, 'but it'll have to be without me on this occasion. Sounds exciting, though. I hope it's a success.' She turned to leave, receiving the distinct impression that Max had overdosed somewhat on powers of persuasion and was using her as a guinea pig for his motivational addresses. The next quarterly meeting should be worth attending to witness another inspirational pep talk, at least in terms of dynamic language, if not on coherent logic and evidence-based substance. She wondered if he had delved into Little Mo for inspiration during his time in Glasgow and was eager to make use of his sales team to practise the principles laid out by the writer.

'Still, you can't make that week, so say no more,' Max continued, his words seemingly communicating the tailing-off of the conversation but the deliberate slowing down of his speech to emphasise the last three words showing he was in no hurry to move on. The effect on Sophie was that she felt obliged to linger just for a few seconds and knew that she would indeed end up saying more than she intended. 'Going anywhere nice?' Max asked, drawing the reply out of the Kent and Sussex representative with consummate skill. Sophie should have known. Max had perfected sales techniques over many years and knew just how to make it emotionally very difficult for his interlocutor to escape without being impolite. Before she knew it she had revealed her destination and that she was going with a male friend. Christmas shopping or sightseeing? Perhaps a bit of both. Keeping her trip to Lisbon low-profile was proving impossible.

When she finally did extricate herself from Max's office, she had hardly gone three steps when she was met by the smiling face of Catherine Holdsworth, who seemed to have overheard at least part of her conversation.

'Going in search of some winter sun, then?' the older woman asked.

'Hopefully,' Sophie replied.

'I am sure this is none of my business, but might it be something to do with a certain young fellow we were discussing at the last quarterly meeting?'

Sophie could only grin wearily and sigh heavily as if to say that for all the warm wishes for her emotional welfare, she could not wait for this topic of conversation to be consigned to history, one way or another. Catherine touched her younger colleague on the elbow supportively and said simply, still grinning, 'I understand. Have a lovely time.'

* * * *

Autumn term at Princewood School duly crawled to its conclusion. After a heavy fortnight of exam marking, report writing, and assisting with end of term events, not least the Year 8 party, the senior rugby dinner at which all the coaches were invited partly to ensure heavy reinforcements in case the sanctioning of alcohol were mismanaged by the sixth formers celebrating the end of the season, the Christmas fayre at which he was obliged to make a purchase, and the rousing end of term carol service in the town's Anglican church, Bear was ready for a break. This last occasion marked the formal end of term and staff were invited to end of term drinks by the Head. Most teachers made an appearance that final Friday afternoon. The unfortunate few would find themselves waylaid by parents with queries about their offspring that they had had all term to ask. Bear was relieved not to be accosted and enjoyed Stephen Rawlinson's hospitality with colleagues.

By now he was past caring about explanations for his forthcoming trip. Again, he found himself in conversation with Claudine, who did not have to probe too deeply to ascertain the identity of his travelling companion.

'I knew eet!' she exclaimed. 'You just 'ave to follow your passion, Grizzly. Life ees too short. I 'ope you 'ave some adventures.'

I do hope not, thought Bear, as he eventually turned his thoughts to recovering over the weekend and preparing himself for what could be a testing week ahead.

Chapter Fifteen
An Expert Verdict

'It's all Björn Bengtsson's fault. He has a lot to answer for,' Bear replied, conscious that he was embarking on much-used phrases, amused that it was only now that Sophie had got around to asking the inevitable question. He paused to elicit the equally predictable follow-up.

'And who's he?' Sophie obliged by asking.

'Lead singer and guitarist for The Cosmics,' Bear answered, deliberately withholding further information with a cheeky grin, as if fully expecting that brief clarification to be sufficient. Momentarily, Sophie wondered if her travelling companion had been speaking to her boss about how to tease her by delaying the release of detail until the last possible moment, but she assumed this was a teacher's storytelling technique, so she played along with it patiently.

'And who are they?' she continued, asking the obvious question.

'You must have heard of The Cosmics?' Bear feigned shock at her ignorance, before deciding to play straight. 'Well, that's not surprising. Not many people have. Rock group that was big, well mildly well known, in the early sixties before they faded away somewhat. Dad was a big fan for a while. He named me after Björn, which, as is widely known, is the Swedish for...'

'Bear?' Sophie completed.

'Exactly. That's the story that has been handed down. He was never into convention, my dad, agreed that Björn would be a bit too pretentious, so my parents named me Bear instead. I gather I had a glare just like Björn when I made my entry into the world. I'm not sure that isn't just part of family mythology. For all I know, it could have been decided as part of a bet down the pub on a Friday night. Something like: if United beat City tomorrow, I'll call my son "Bear".'

Sophie chuckled. 'What if you'd been a girl?'

'Apparently, I would have been Ursula, which means little bear. My dad said that would have been fine by him, but I'm not sure my mum would have been happy; she's never taken to the name.'

They both smiled. Now half an hour into their flight from London Gatwick to Lisbon, the travelling companions had started to relax after their early morning journey via underground and surface rail to the airport in time for the departure of the 8.30 a.m. flight. Bear in particular had sacrificed sleep to drive to Camden to meet Sophie in the small hours to accompany her to Gatwick, south of London. A partially energising coffee and croissant in the departure lounge had compensated for sleep deprivation and now, above the coast of Brittany, they both started to reflect on the bizarre circumstances of their adventure. Bear had asked Sophie on at least three occasions where she was keeping the brooch, and she assured him that the precious cargo was staying in her hand luggage at all costs. She admonished him on his last enquiry that walls had ears and suggested a code for communicating. 'The horse is in the stable' was her assurance that she had not forgotten or misplaced the very reason for their visit. She smiled at the subterfuge they felt compelled to adopt but her musing was interrupted by Bear pursuing the theme of names.

'None of the children at school are sure of my real name,' he said. 'Some have heard other teachers calling me Bear but assume it's a nickname. I've never had to tell them the whole truth... yet.'

'I suppose you hardly need a nickname with a name like Bear,' observed Sophie.

'One of my colleagues calls me Grizzly, but you could hardly say she calls me Grizzly for short. How about you? Any interesting nicknames?'

'Oh, just Bingo.'

'Bingo?'

'From my surname. Bingham. That was my name at school for years. Now it's just plain Sophie, or Soph, if you love abbreviations like my boss Max.'

'Bear and Bingo boldly brave the Baixa,' Bear declared, searching for an amusing alliteration, instinctively throwing in the name of the Lisbon district where they would be staying that night.

* * * *

The choice of accommodation in the Baixa, or lower town, was quite deliberate. Being situated in the heart of the city, it housed many of the country's administrative departments, including the Instituto de Cultura Nacional. After a bus ride from the airport deposited them to their hotel early that afternoon, Bear and Sophie decided to locate the attractive nineteenth-century building that was just a couple of blocks away, in readiness for their audience with Senhor Cardoso the following day. They wished to leave nothing to chance by risking being late. Once this key landmark had been identified, the pair, without needing to articulate such a desire, decided that with hours to kill, some attempt at tourism was in order. The starting point of the Baixa was particularly attractive to Sophie, with a grid of pedestrianised streets containing traditional crafts such as silverware, cobblers and wooden items. The lure of street performers and pavement artists distracted both travellers as they strolled through the district. Bear had read about the inception of the grid system, instituted by the king's commissioned architect Plombal to rebuild the city centre after the horrendous earthquake of 1755. The neat arrangement of streets expressed simplicity and precision, economising space in the heart of the capital. The distinct design must have been a symbol of hope, or at least a new beginning, as the city began to be rebuilt.

Sophie took Bear's dreamy silence for lack of interest in the district and decided it was time for his one expressed desire to be fulfilled.

'Come on, then. Enough of shops for now,' she said purposefully, 'castle time.'

Bear had indeed earmarked the Castelo de Sao Jorge as a site of interest. A short bus ride took them to the imposing monument with spectacular views over the city and the River Tejo.

They wandered around the medieval quarter of Santa Cruz and took an enjoyable ramble along the ramparts amid tolerable winter sunshine, the temperature a few degrees higher than in London. Bear was mentally forming a picture of the city as it might have looked in 1147 when a group of passing Crusaders was persuaded to stop by and liberate

Lisbon from the Moors. This they accomplished, by all accounts, with unbridled savagery. There was just time to take in the old, poorer Mouraria quarter, the district to which the Moors were confined after the sack of the city. Borders within cities, with Jewish and Muslim quarters, Bear reflected, were not the sole preserve of Lisbon. He wondered whether he was doing anything to break down barriers or simply reinforcing them by endorsing a society where wealth and material comfort dictated lifestyle more than he cared to admit. In another pensive moment, he started to question why they were here in Portugal that week. Was it just to ensure that Sophie's brooch fetched a proper price? Or to satisfy a taste for adventure? Somehow, the phrase 'unfinished business', would not leave him. He needed his companion to jolt him back to the present and return his thoughts to mundane matters of eating out and getting a much-needed night's rest.

* * * *

'The horse is in the stable, before you ask,' Sophie assured Bear, applying the pre-arranged code as they stepped outside their hotel at a quarter past nine the following morning. Although she was carrying a handbag, Bear knew the stable to refer to an inside coat pocket, safe from any possible pickpockets or bag-snatchers. Unsurprisingly, the day's exertions and the early start caught up with them, causing them both to retire early, not before Bear succeeded in eliciting some information about public transport from the reception desk. Refreshed by sleep, they headed around the corner to 60, Rua dos Sapateiros, site of the Instituto de Cultura Nacional.

For no particular reason, Bear had assumed that such an

official building with a definitively authoritative title would be quite palatial, with massive stone pillars either side of a wide entrance. In fact, as they had ascertained the previous day, it was quite unassuming. A simple two-storey building with a single plaque outside announcing its purpose, it blended into the everyday bustle of the Baixa. It covered the space of perhaps a large detached house in width, and housed several offices plus a medium-sized lecture hall designed to host select gatherings rather than vast assemblies with standing room only. There was no need for the Instituto to be pretentious: it served as the authority on aspects of the nation's history and its experts worked from offices in the building when not lecturing at the city's university. The Instituto did not keep many relics on site. Hence security was limited to one guard patrolling relatively discreetly outside. Bear and Sophie entered the main door that was accessible from the pedestrianised street and walked up to a reception desk where they were greeted by a woman of roughly their own age, neatly turned out in white blouse and red necktie.

'Bom dia,' she said.

'Bom dia,' replied Bear in his deliberately prepared Portuguese. *'Fala ingles?'*

'A little,' the receptionist replied with a weak smile.

Prepared for such an eventuality, Bear produced a sheet of notepaper from his pocket, on which were inscribed his and Sophie's surnames, that of Senhor Cardoso and the time of appointment. 'We have an appointment with Senhor Cardoso,' he said slowly.

The receptionist acknowledged the validity of the request, made a telephone call and gestured for the visitors to take a seat on a sofa with its back to the wall. They did so and spent what felt much longer than the two minutes that it was in reality in nervous silence. There was no more speculation to be done; they had arrived at their destination, and the verdict on the bronze ornament was imminent. They glanced at the wall on which posters hung that referred to exhibitions held under the auspices of the institute, and another which seemed to give dates of forthcoming events. In a glass case there was a photograph of a man receiving some kind of award from what looked like a city mayor or similar civic dignitary, if it could be judged by the sash and chain the official was wearing. Enthusiastic applause and smiles decorated the background as this ceremony was obviously a popular award. The transparent atmosphere of celebration for this success, presumably of someone attached to the institute, was curiously at odds with the quiet and business-like, rather dull surroundings. Otherwise vast areas of the walls were bare, as if designed to dampen any fervour of visitors expecting any exciting revelations.

After two minutes a short, middle-aged woman entered from behind the reception desk and addressed the visitors in clear, if heavily accented English. 'Mr Hoskins? Miss Bingham? Good morning, welcome to the Instituto. My name is Rosa De Freitas. I am Senhor Cardoso's assistant. You have come a long way. Did you have a pleasant flight?'

'Yes, thank you,' replied Sophie.

'Please follow me,' Rosa De Freitas continued, indicating that that was the extent of any small talk. She led them along a corridor, up a flight of stairs and turned left on to another corridor, where she knocked on the second door. On hearing a response from within, she ushered the visitors in to meet the jewellery expert. 'Senhor Cardoso will see you now,' she gestured at a man in a grey suit who was seated behind a desk.

Manuel Cardoso was a fit man for his sixty-five years. He rose from his chair with an agility of someone half his age and strode forward to greet his visitors. Of medium build, he took care of his appearance, with a neatly trimmed grey beard and rimless spectacles complementing his formal attire. When Bear was close enough to notice, he noted that the dark green tie Cardoso sported carried the initials ICN, with some form of heraldic emblem above the lettering. Clearly this was a man who was proud of the institution he represented and embraced the responsibilities the post presented. Rosa closed the door behind her, and the academic greeted his clients.

'Good morning, Mr Hoskins, Miss Bingham,' he said in correct, carefully chosen English, 'welcome to the Instituto de Cultura Nacional. I hope you have had a pleasant journey from London?'

'Yes, thank you,' Sophie replied.

'Very pleasant,' Bear added, 'it's very good of you to see us.'

'It is my pleasure. Please...' said Cardoso, gesturing to hard-backed chairs facing his desk, inviting his guests to be seated as he resumed his position sitting opposite them. 'I read your letter with much interest, Mr Hoskins. I receive many letters. People ask if an object is genuine, you see. Is it worth lots of money? Many times, I have to disappoint them. From what you say this may be different.' Cardoso took pains to emphasise the word 'may'.

Manuel Cardoso was reluctant to reveal his hand straight away. When he received Bear's letter, he felt a surge of excitement and made sure his diary was clear that Tuesday morning, just in case his optimism was justified. He had been there before, of course. Clients had been referred to him to verify whether precious items discovered in a loft or uncovered in a family move or house clearance really dated back to the post-Restoration period of Portuguese history from 1640, when the country regained independence from Spain. Invariably he had been obliged to conclude that the work was that of a much later forgery. He had for many years been the country's expert on the jewellery of that period and was employed three days a week at the institute, giving consultations, writing for the monthly journal, preparing exhibitions that the institute organised and were shown at museums in Lisbon and around the country. His expertise was also called upon for incoming and outgoing museum loans, and his work had taken him to Paris, New York and London, where his details had been noted for future reference by staff at the British Museum. He still lectured on sixteenth- and seventeenth-century Iberian history at the university and kept his mind active through writing articles on the period.

'So,' he continued, 'you have a brooch with a horseman?'

'Yes,' Sophie answered, reaching into her inside pocket and extracting the item from an envelope. 'I bought it in Valença do Minho in the summer and we think, at least my friend found out, it might be worth much more than I paid for it.'

She placed the brooch on the desk. Cardoso nodded, picked it up and studied it carefully.

He nodded again to himself and then said, 'Aha. *Unita fortior*. Interesting,' in reference to the Latin motto. He picked up a magnifying glass and slowly passed it along the surface of the brooch, examining all the contours meticulously.

'There seem to be some waves in the background,' Bear

tried to explain.

'Not waves, flames. As I would expect,' said the expert without looking up. He then did something that his guests had not anticipated. He slowly turned the brooch over and applied the magnifying glass to the back of the object. 'Aha,' he repeated, and picked up a ballpoint pen from a jar on the desk and began to note some letters down on a writing pad. He had to examine the brooch from different angles because the fastening, added at a later date, was obscuring his vision. After about a minute of checking he turned to his visitors with a smile of cautious satisfaction. 'One moment, please,' he said, and rose to delve into a filing cabinet to his left, from which he extracted a file. Bear and Sophie exchanged puzzled glances and felt rising tension as the expert placed his scrap of paper alongside a document in the file. His eyes moved from one piece of paper to the other, making some form of comparison.

'Incrível!' he exclaimed before finally looking up, directing an astonished stare at both his visitors. For a moment he added nothing more, then repeated, 'One moment please' and reached for the telephone on his desk. In the briefest of calls Bear and Sophie heard Rosa's name mentioned, and twenty seconds later Cardoso's assistant re-entered the room. Cardoso said a few words to her in Portuguese, the meaning of which she relayed.

'Senhor Cardoso has asked me to translate from now on,' Rosa explained, not the least put out by the request, as if she anticipated such an eventuality.

'When I am excited,' Cardoso continued briefly in English, 'I need to say it in Portuguese.' He then resumed in his native language at a rapid rate before straining to slow down for the benefit of his interpreter. Bear could not resist a wry smile; the contrast to Herod dispensing with the services of his interpreter came immediately to mind.

Rosa pulled up a chair and translated the expert's words in chunks of two or three sentences. 'Senhor Cardoso says he is ninety-nine per cent certain this brooch is part of a set of four. They date from the early- to mid-seventeenth century... They were crafted as a symbol of resistance by families of Portuguese nobles during the period of Spanish rule that ended with restoration of independence in 1640. The brooches would have been worn by the ladies of these families on certain public occasions... All four have horsemen on the front and they represent the Four Horsemen of the Apocalypse, from the book of Revelation at the end of the Bible. They symbolise conquest, war, famine and death...'

'Hardly the sort of thing you would give your lady friend for her birthday, I would have thought?' Bear remarked, adding momentary levity to the proceedings. Rosa started to translate but Cardoso indicated he got the gist of the question and resumed his explanation.

'The less pleasant images are concealed,' Rosa continued her translation. 'What the lady would see was a gallant horseman, armed, fighting off danger. The motto *'Unita fortior'* is seen above the picture in all four brooches. It is only in the background that we see other images... In this one we see flames. They represent war, a conflagration. In another brooch, the one representing death, we see a tiny picture of a skull... Normally the four horses would be distinguished by different colours: a white horse for conquest, a red horse for war, a black horse for famine and an ashen horse for death.... Of course, on a bronze brooch these colours could not be shown, but the images in the background make it clear which horseman is represented...The intricate craftsmanship indicates that this brooch is part of a set of four and would almost certainly be worth well in excess of the sum you mentioned in your letter, probably ten times as much...'

Bear and Sophie sat open-mouthed as they took in the assistant's translation.

'But...' Sophie hesitantly asked, 'how can you be absolutely sure it's genuine, Senhor Cardoso? It may be great craftsmanship, but is it genuine?'

Again, Cardoso understood the question but proceeded with his explanation in his native tongue.

'From the back of the brooch. There is a tiny inscription in Latin on each of the four brooches. They were a sort of code known only to the families and their supporters... Each inscription is part of a sentence... Senhor Cardoso has a translation of three of the inscriptions... That is, the first, third and fourth parts of the sentence... the back of the first brooch reads, "From the valley of despair"... The third says, "that will purify our people"... The fourth says, "and will dispel the enemy"... These three brooches have been found... The second brooch has never been found... until now... The words on the back of the brooch you brought in today read, "spring forth streams of hope". It completes the sentence.'

Bear and Sophie sat perplexed, excited yet still puzzled as to how each of these jigsaw pieces could fit together.

'But how,' Bear asked slowly and deliberately, 'can we know that someone didn't just invent the second bit of the sentence to make it fit in and pass a fake brooch off as genuine?'

'That would be impossible,' Rosa transmitted Cardoso's response that was delivered with a knowing smile. 'The other three are known to the National Museum and are regularly displayed at exhibitions. But the back of the brooch is never shown… Until now I was the only person who knew the content of the rest of the sentence… Now there are just the four of us.'

Cardoso let the words of the translation sink in before he took Bear aback by addressing him in English, and by the nature of his question.

'Tell me, Mr Hoskins, are you a religious man?'

Bear strove always to avoid using that adjective in describing himself but decided not to overcomplicate things.

'Yes, I am a Christian, a believer,' he said simply.

'I am a Catholic. I have a strong faith, but there are many things I cannot explain. Let me say something. I will need Rosa's help again.' He reverted to Portuguese and Rosa resumed her duties.

'Senhor Cardoso read once about prophecies… Someone suggested that Jesus Christ could have fulfilled prophecies about himself by accident… That he wasn't the promised Messiah, but just by chance he was the only person in history who fulfilled prophecies by accidentally, unknowingly, doing what was prophesised centuries before… For example, riding into Jerusalem on a donkey, as the prophet Zechariah foretold… It has been calculated that the probability of Jesus fulfilling just eight prophecies by chance was one in one hundred million billion…' Rosa was obliged to pause as Cardoso let his words be digested before continuing. 'Whatever your beliefs, that gives you an idea of how unlikely some forgery is. In this case I would say the odds of faking the missing fourth brooch details are very similar… It is as near impossible as you can imagine.'

'But why four brooches?' asked Bear. 'Could there be

more than four?'

'Very unlikely, unless the writer wanted lots of long subordinate clauses... Don't forget there are four horsemen of the apocalypse... It was reckoned that the use of them as symbols indicated judgement and an end to a system of government, in this case Spanish rule after sixty years... Four in the Bible is seen as a number of completion: four directions of north, south, east and west... The book of Revelation talks of four living creatures round the throne of God and heaven containing men and women of every tribe and language and people and nation...' At this point Cardoso used his fingers to count the four nouns mentioned. 'There are many other examples. I am convinced there are four brooches and that this brooch is the missing one.'

'So where are the other three?' asked Sophie.

'That I cannot tell you,' said Cardoso through his interpreter. 'They belong to a private individual. I gather he lends them to the museum from time to time. All I know is that he lives outside Lisbon.'

'He?' pressed Sophie. 'So you know it's a man, at least?'

'I'm sorry,' Cardoso clarified via Rosa, 'it's just a manner of speaking. I meant "he or she". I don't even know if it's a man or a woman... This person wishes to remain anonymous. Only one or two people at the museum know who this person is. If you want to contact him or her, I'm afraid you will be disappointed.'

'That's not a problem,' Bear responded, casting a knowing glance towards Sophie, 'I have a pretty good idea who we're talking about.'

Chapter Sixteen
Guarda

The city of Guarda is distinctive in being at once forbidding and fascinating. Some five hours' train journey to the northeast of Lisbon, its location on the edge of the Serra da Estrela, the mountain range in the Beira Alta region, affords some spectacular views that would lure tourists in reasonable numbers in warmer months. In December, however, a decision to stay in Guarda would need considerable deliberation and forethought. True, as a medieval city, founded in 1197 to guard the country's borders against both the Moors and the Spaniards, Guarda is not without historical interest. Anyone poring over guidebooks will soon discover that the city is known by the four fs—*fria, farta, forte* and *feia*—cold, rich, strong and ugly. As a fortress town that was previously much closer to the border, it undeniably needed to be a place of strength. The first and last adjectives seemed designed to put off the faint-hearted traveller. Reputed to be the highest city in Europe with an altitude over 1,000 metres, it is certainly cold and windswept virtually all year round. A visit to Guarda in mid-December is strictly for the connoisseur.

Bear Hoskins could justifiably lay claim to being a connoisseur in matters relating to borders. He had certainly not been lacking in deliberation and forethought ever since he had picked up Pedro Gomes' business card a few days after their encounter in Camden and realised that the antiques dealer lived in Guarda. After initially taking no more than half-hearted interest in the location, his passion was ignited once the return trip to Portugal was planned, and especially as it became clear to him and Sophie that paying a visit to Pedro was in order. This, surely, was a border visit for the connoisseur: going to a city with a rich past but a gloomy appearance, well away from the capital and the very end of the railway line, to boot. A border town that retained its appearance as such, even though the actual frontier now lay some twenty miles to the east. He had devoured the relevant section of his guidebook that recommended savouring the exterior of the cathedral, whose gargoyles were a notable feature, the ones facing eastwards to Spain supposedly appearing particularly menacing. He was looking forward to that 'end of the world' sensation at two-fifteen that Tuesday afternoon in Lisbon as the train moved out of Santa Apolónia station on its journey north.

As the suburbs gave way to the rolling countryside, the two travellers sat facing each other and reflected on the events of the morning. The consultation with Manuel Cardoso had turned out to be relatively brief and business-like, the academic's explanation of the Four Horsemen of the Apocalypse notwithstanding. They had thanked Manuel, as he insisted on being called, and Rosa for their help, and promised to keep them informed of any further developments. Manuel's parting advice that they should not openly discuss the item in question nor display it in public seemed as if he were stating the obvious, but it was delivered with such careful, earnest deliberation that the message sunk into the consciousness of his visitors.

Conversation between Bear and Sophie was equally brief and purposeful as they left the Instituto to return to their hotel. They both knew that the next move was to try to track Pedro down. A phone call in advance would ascertain whether the dealer was at home that week but alerting him of a forthcoming visit might pose dangers if Pedro was involved in any illegal racket. If their suspicions proved correct, he was indeed the mysterious owner of the remaining three brooches and regularly loaned them out to the National Museum and clearly had an interest in acquiring the fourth. He would, therefore, be known to the museum and easy to locate if anything untoward were taking place. Unless, of course, he was using a go-between to cover his tracks, as D'Oliveira had done.

Having checked the train times the night before Bear knew they could comfortably make the afternoon service for Guarda. There was even time for Sophie to take the initiative, extract her mobile phone and with rudimentary Portuguese, book two hotel rooms in Guarda near the cathedral close to the top of the hill with the most stunning views over the mountain range. This was a move that took Bear by surprise. He had a standard, bemused, almost contemptuous remark that he threw into conversation whenever the topic of emerging mobile communication was raised. He revelled in exposing the supposed banality and vanity of travellers announcing that they were on the train, just about to leave the train or inform someone that the train was on time. Otherwise he saw little use for such intrusive technology. He had even gone as far as to say he would never purchase such a device and amongst his colleagues he had a ready audience for such quips. For the first time, having witnessed the efficiency with which his companion had executed the required accommodation arrangements, he felt forced to rethink. Maybe an idea for the future, he mused and immediately shelved the thought. Now, with the luxury of a few hours before their next move, they began to mull over their situation.

'I suppose it's a case of being flexible and responding to whatever happens,' Sophie pondered after they had taken their seats facing each other in the train.

'The key thing is to get some idea as to Pedro's true intentions,' Bear replied. 'Which will be a lot easier if he is at home and we meet him in person.'

'If he isn't, we can try and make some enquiries. I'm not sure how far we'll get, what with the language barrier, but we might pick up a few clues as to how he does business.'

'That won't give us much time to hunt around Guarda trying to root out evidence on Pedro's character.'

'As you say, flexibility is the key.'

They were silent for a few moments, before Sophie continued.

'What did you make of Pedro?' This was not the first time she had asked Bear his opinion on the subject but felt the need to repeat the question in the light of their meeting that morning.

'Well, I was about to say a typical salesman, could talk the hind legs off a donkey,' Bear replied with a cheeky grin, 'but I'd better not dig myself in deeper before you throw something at me.'

Sophie seemed uninterested in any jovial jousting about her occupation and maintained a serious tone. 'I mean, when we met him in Camden, all right, he was chatty and pushy at first, he pushed his luck all right, but normally in sales you know when you're not going to win. You engage with the potential customer, you use charm, you're polite and bubbly, feign interest in the person you're talking to without making it seem too blatant... but when it's clear the other person isn't interested, you give up, win some, lose some, on to the next one. He didn't do that.'

'I know. He followed us to the pub,' Bear recalled.

'But there was a desperation in his eyes, almost pleading. You don't get that even if you want to make a deal really badly. He said that it was really important for him and...'

'And what?'

'Well, I thought he said it was "really important for me and my"...'

'My what?' asked Bear, puzzled.

'I thought, I may be wrong, but I thought he was about to say, "my family". I can't be sure, that's just intuition, I guess, but he never got the chance to finish his sentence.' Sophie directed a mildly admonishing smile at Bear.

'I know,' confessed Bear, 'that must have been when I cut in and was quite short with him.'

'At least you may get the chance to apologise to him,' said Sophie with a smile.

After another thoughtful pause Sophie resumed. 'But we have to check him out. If the bro... the horse in our stable,' she corrected herself, with a furtive glance over her shoulder, 'is part of a set of four, and they are being used as a museum display, I suppose we have almost a moral obligation to make it available... to the world.' She added the last phrase reflectively, scarcely able to take in the potential enormity of the find.

'You would have to negotiate your price if that's the case,' commented Bear.

'That business about four was interesting, wasn't it?' she said, changing the course of the conversation suddenly.

'What business?' asked Bear.

'You know, what Manuel said about the number four. About it being a number of significance. What did he say, that four is the number of...?'

'Completion,' Bear completed her sentence in timely fashion.

'That's it, completion. So there can only be four horsemen and we've got the missing link, possibly. Or probably. Did you know all that before? Do they go into all that revelation stuff in your church?'

Bear chuckled. 'Occasionally. I was only vaguely aware of the four horsemen. I think if our minister spent too long in the book of Revelation, he'd lose the whole congregation. It's such a complicated book. But Manuel sounded as if he could go on for hours. He's obviously done lots of research.'

'Hmm. It sounds a bit spooky to me... but in a funny way, sort of inspirational, you know, getting families to rally round in a gesture of national unity.'

'Perhaps there are other commemorative items from the period worth investigating,' Bear observed and immediately realised he had donned his historian's hat and lost his companion in the process. They were silent again before Sophie returned them to more seasonal topics of conversation.

'So are you all ready for Christmas?' she asked, grinning. 'That was a joke, by the way.'

'I was about to say that this year I've hardly got around to thinking about it,' replied Bear. 'But knowing this week was coming up, I had a busy day shopping last Saturday, just after term finished. Usually I collapse in a heap when we break up, but this time I hit the shops. Finding something for my niece and nephew took a while, but I got there in the end. How about you? All set?'

'I always do Christmas shopping in November before everywhere gets too crowded.' They exchanged details of holiday plans. Bear was heading to his parents in Carlisle for Christmas, looking forward to a windswept stroll along Hadrian's Wall if the weather didn't prove too inclement and had an invitation to call on Angela and Martin over New Year. Mac had made a suggestion of New Year's Eve at The Anchor, which didn't sound too original, and Bear was considering his options. Sophie was spending the festive period with her mother, who lived with her partner near Reading, and was undecided as to her plans for the New Year. It was when Sophie asked Bear if he had any special events or parties to attend that Bear reached for the inside pocket of the coat that he had placed in the overhead rack. He extracted a set of paper invitation cards, wrapped together in a rubber band. They had become rather crumpled from the exertions of travel over the past few days.

'I almost forgot,' he said before clarifying, 'well, I did forget, completely slipped my mind. I have some invitations that I promised to try to get given out.'

'Ooh… is it to a party?' Sophie asked playfully.

'Not as exciting as that,' said Bear, then corrected himself, 'well, you never know, it could be really exciting. Something I'm taking part in on Sunday.'

He handed her a paper ticket, which she took and studied with interest. While Bear qualified his invitation by saying that Sophie would probably be too tired and have better things to do that afternoon, but just in case, he had to fulfil his duty in publicising the event. If Bear expected a typically British polite refusal, or a non-committal promise to give the matter thought, he was surprised by her immediate response to the invitation:

Grove Street Baptist Church, Princewood
warmly invite you to a Christmas spectacular:
The Joy of Four
a nativity play, with carols for the whole family
Sunday, _th December 199_, 3.30 p.m.
Entry free
Mince pies, tea, coffee and mulled wine afterwards

'It's that number again, isn't it?' She looked up to cast Bear a disarming look.

'Number?' queried Bear.

'Number four. Like Manuel was talking about four representing completing things. Here it is again. Why four? Does that mean there's going to be a lot of stuff about Revelation?'

'Oh, I see. I think it's because it's the fourth Sunday in Advent and the period before Christmas will be complete by then.' Bear vaguely recollected Cynthia explaining some relevance to the time of year as the reasoning behind the title of the event. Truth be told, he hadn't paid much attention to the title, and although, along with other members of the congregation and cast, he had taken several invitations to distribute, he had been too preoccupied to make the effort to do so until now. His conscience was now partially pacified by his half-hearted presentation of a crumpled ticket to his fellow passenger.

'And how does Bear Hoskins fit into this spectacular?'

199

Sophie asked.

'Oh, I'm Melchior… one of the three wise men. I'm acting the part, and singing a solo, would you believe? That's probably why I have been so slow to hand out the invites. My singing is something I would not wish on anyone.'

'I can imagine you as a singer. I'm sure there's some melody beneath that gruff bear exterior.'

That last comment, though meant to be light-hearted and complimentary, took Bear aback somewhat. He was left to ponder whether he really did come across as gruff, almost hostile. He knew he did not have the most effervescent of personalities, neither the flamboyance of Peter Walton or Claudine Leblanc, nor the jovial bonhomie of John Billington, nor the effusive enthusiasm of Rachel Rhodes. He was just studious, careful, reflective Bear. That was his style, in the classroom and without. He did not know whether he could change that, or want to, if he tried. Maybe first appearances can be off-putting, he thought, as conversation died down and he and Sophie buried themselves in books for a while. Probably, he concluded with a wry smile to himself, he would never have developed any sort of connection with Sophie had it not been for the prolonged rain in Valença encouraging a much lengthier dialogue than he would otherwise have initiated. After some twenty minutes or so, Sophie announced that she would try to get forty winks before their journey finished. Bear reminded her that, since Guarda was the terminus, it wouldn't be a disaster if they both fell asleep; they could linger in their seats without the danger of missing their stop. With that assurance, Sophie closed her eyes and attempted to catch up on sleep.

* * * *

Pedro Gomes rose from his seat and moved along the compartment in the direction of the toilet, roughly ninety minutes from the end of the journey. It had been a demanding visit to Lisbon as he sought to achieve sales on some antiques whose origins could not be verified, and he had met with only limited success. He was looking forward to a relaxing end of the week at home before attending two more pre-Christmas markets at the weekend. Trade had hardly been brisk in the past few weeks, but at least the forces of law and order had not paid any further visits and they seemed convinced that any connection he had with Eduardo D'Oliveira was tenuous, at worst.

He approached the end of the carriage and noticed that the toilet was occupied, so rather than waiting, decided to stretch his legs along the carriage for the next available facilities. He was about to enter the adjoining compartment when his attention was drawn to a figure resting her head on a rolled-up raincoat on the window seat facing the direction of travel. She was wearing a bright yellow woollen pullover and her light brown wavy hair drew instant recognition. Even with her eyes closed she was clearly recognisable. Pedro reacted with a stifled gasp of excitement mingled with fear. He had wondered more than once since October how he would handle meeting the 'brooch pair', as he termed them, again, without ever imagining that such an encounter would materialise. Cautiously craning his neck to the left as though looking for someone, he quickly cast a glance sideways to ascertain what he assumed to be true. His expectation was justified. Opposite the young woman was the dark-haired man of medium height who had ended up being confrontational at the London pub that afternoon. Sophia and Ben, or whatever their names were, were on the train and heading, presumably, towards Guarda. That could mean only one intention: to arrange a meeting with himself.

Swiftly retreating to pursue other washroom arrangements, Pedro found the original toilet now vacant and disappeared inside. Having relieved himself, he stared at an anxious face in the mirror for some moments, trying to make sense of his discovery. He heard the rattle of the door and realised he needed to return to his seat. The last thing he wanted to do was to bump into this Ben character in the corridor and renew acquaintance. He quickly exited and found his window seat again. Fortunately, he reasoned, he was located well into his carriage and there was little likelihood of either of these individuals heading his way for the duration of the journey. Why, he thought to himself, was he so concerned, almost fearful, of meeting this pair of travellers again? Assuming the woman was still in possession of the brooch, this was surely a godsend; an unexpected second chance to purchase the brooch he coveted so much. Had they come to Guarda for such a purpose? Surely, they were not contemplating a winter holiday in the region? From their conversation at the market in London, he knew that she, at least, was no stranger to the country, but making a second visit in so short a time span made little sense. They clearly meant to meet up with him, presumably to arrange a sale. His adrenaline rushed faster as he considered the prospect. He knew he could not afford to let this unique opportunity slip through his fingers.

Yet the excitement was tempered by a profound disquiet

as he recalled the details of his encounter with the couple. Indeed, they could hardly be termed a couple; at no time in their conversation had he detected any term of endearment being offered between them. There was no physical contact, no sense in their body language or gaze that they were lovers. When he had decided to tail them as they headed towards a pub, he had been scrupulously careful to maintain as discreet a distance as possible, terrified of one of them turning around and immediately spotting him and denouncing his ploy. To his relief they did not, but at no time in the walk to the pub did they hold hands or show any sign of intimacy. Why, then, were they travelling together now? As he considered the answer to his own question, there was a rustling in the corridor as a passenger sought to get past. Pedro rapidly grasped at his newspaper and virtually buried himself in its pages until the passenger passed, mercifully neither of the pair he was trying to avoid. He drew a quizzical look from the woman sitting diagonally opposite him in the aisle seat, who clearly thought his behaviour to be peculiar. I can hardly blame her, he thought. Pull yourself together, Pedro, you can't be as jumpy as this for the next hour and a half. He resolved to respond as honestly as possible if the pair did approach him between now and Guarda.

His mind would not rest, however. He ruefully recalled how he had handled the situation that October Saturday. He had seen them enter the pub and deliberately waited along the street for a good quarter of an hour, choosing a vantage point that enabled him to be sure that they had not had second thoughts and left to find an alternative hostelry. When convinced that they were settled, he had chanced his arm and made what he now recognised was a pretty unconvincing attempt at pretending to stumble across them by chance in entering the pub. He was certain they were not fooled. He recollected their interaction with each other yet again. Two fit young people, who were not intimately involved and did not seem to know each other well. Certainly not related. Colleagues? They presumably worked together. Pedro could not shake off the improbable, but not implausible, conclusion that they were in the police. Plain clothes investigators. Just before the news of the D'Oliveira arrest broke. It made sense. Maybe they had been tracing him for a while and deliberately lured him to the pub, fully expecting to be followed. Were they gathering evidence of any dealers from the north of Portugal? But if so, why had this Ben character reacted so aggressively when I was about to produce my business card?

Had he thought I was about to put cash on the table? Why didn't he draw me out more so that they had something incriminating to work on? Maybe they were just happy once they had located me and decided not to pursue me for the moment. Until now.

The remainder of the journey was profoundly uncomfortable for the antiques dealer. He needed to buy himself time to prepare a response for the foreign visitors, as he concluded that a visit was imminent. As the train drew into Guarda, he headed to the exit door of his carriage to be the first to alight. Anticipating that the British pair would take a few moments to get their bearings and establish their next move, possibly to work out how to find some means of onward transport, he determined to be first on to the platform and out through the entrance hall before being spotted. His plan was executed flawlessly, and he reached the sanctuary of his car without encountering either of his supposed pursuers.

* * * *

Since their accommodation near the cathedral called itself a *residencial* rather than a *pensão* or a hotel, Bear and Sophie did not receive breakfast there. They paid simply for the night's sleep. The limited facilities, however, did not inconvenience them in any way as they were not bound to a set time for rising when they awoke the following morning. Whilst a degree of detective work was anticipated during the day that necessitated making the most of the restricted daylight hours, the travellers agreed that any attempt to check out breakfast options before nine o'clock would not be in order. They both needed to recover from the latest travel exertions before facing the demands of a winter Wednesday in Guarda. Consequently, when Bear knocked on Sophie's door with reliable precision at a minute past nine, she was already up and ready to face the challenges of the day, commenting on her companion's consistent punctuality.

They soon discovered a café on the main square and breakfasted on coffee, herbal tea, cheese rolls and pastries, ensuring they were well fortified for the tasks ahead. Bear acknowledged that they needed to identify where Pedro lived sooner rather than later, although he had been looking forward to exploring the cathedral and the views across the valley. A winter twilight on a fine day would be spectacular. Yet he realised no time could be lost if this part of their travels was to prove meaningful. The residencial, being a functional establishment simply providing keys and linen, could not help with providing access to a telephone directory. The tourist information office was the next option. Situated just off the main square, the visitors sought it out immediately after breakfast, only to learn that in winter it did not open until ten a.m. That gave Bear the opportunity to lead Sophie through the cobbled streets and narrow alleys of the old town to one of the most striking viewpoints, looking south-west to the Serra da Estrela. There was a chill wind adding to the noticeably colder temperature than in Lisbon, and they realised that keeping on the move for a few minutes to stay warm was definitely in order. As their brief wander brought them back to the cathedral, they were able from this approach to notice for the first time how the dour grey stonework contrasted with the red rooftops and the brighter façades of buildings surrounding it. It was as though the cathedral, as well as the fortified city itself, was making a proud statement of defiance, or at least of self-identity to the world. Bear was about to make a further reference to the four fs that traditionally describe Guarda as strong, ugly, rich and cold, but then recalled reading on the train that the civic leaders had instituted a campaign to change the four fs to five. *Feia*, ugly, was to be replaced by *fiel* (faithful) and *formosa* (beautiful). Observing the well-proportioned, sturdy edifice and the spacious square in front of him, Bear reflected that such an amendment, while more of a mouthful, was far from unjustified.

On entering the tourist office at two minutes past ten, they were greeted warmly by a cheerful middle-aged woman dressed in a smart white blouse, green necktie and navy-blue skirt. Bear had to suppress a smile as he observed that Foundation Books seemed to have branched out into continental operations all of a sudden. His momentary glance at Sophie was not reciprocated; such uniforms must be all too commonplace in that field that she scarcely noticed, or more probably, was too preoccupied with the task at hand to spot similarities in fashion.

Sophie confidently addressed the employee with the usual *'Fala ingles?'* On this occasion they were informed that communication would have to proceed in the local tongue.

'English this afternoon. Two o'clock,' the woman cheerily articulated with a carefully rehearsed English response as if announcing the start of a tea dance or similar entertainment to look forward to. Clearly the tourist office was not expecting British visitors this far up country in the midst of winter.

Realising that waiting until the Anglophone colleague appeared for his or her shift would delay matters, the two visitors, through broken Portuguese, gestures and the help of a pocket dictionary, succeeded in communicating their wish to see a local telephone directory. Bear was about to produce Pedro's business card to demonstrate their trustworthiness as friends of the dealer, but then thought better of it, not knowing whether recent wariness of the jewellery trade had reached these parts. The directory was then produced, and the two companions took seats near a display of information leaflets around a coffee table. They proceeded to try to locate the address of P. Gomes. They had already discussed that this task might take a while with such a common surname, tantamount to locating a Smith or Jones in Britain. The anticipated patience was indeed called for, as Bear was obliged on two occasions to adjust his chair's position to accommodate a customer behind him who was trying to access the leaflets. Over fifty entries under the name of Gomes were in the directory, and twelve with the initial P. Finally, the address that matched Pedro's number was identified.

'Eureka!' exclaimed Sophie. She proceeded to write down

the address in her diary and advanced to the counter to ask the employee where such a street was to be found. From immediate recognition of the information and the careful explanation she received, she perceived that the address was about fifteen minutes' walk down the hill, just outside the old town. The route was helpfully marked for her on a map of the town and she felt a tingling sensation that she had virtually reached journey's end. It was almost a formality to glance at her companion as if to ask whether they should set off now. Bear voiced the rationale that they both knew represented the most logical course of action.

'There may be no one at home, but the sooner we look, the more likely we are to find some answers before we fly back.'

They thanked the employee profusely and exited the tourist office. With the aid of the town map, they descended the hill, through the narrow streets and one of the picturesque portals into a more modern neighbourhood. As predicted, within a quarter of an hour they had alighted upon the residential street they were looking for.

Chapter Seventeen
The Missing Peace

Luisa Gomes rose sharply to her feet in response to the doorbell. Not too quickly, don't look too keen or too nervous, she told herself and deliberately regulated her pace towards the front door. She had been given specific instructions by her husband when he returned from his business trip the previous evening. She had hoped not to need to carry them out in the event of Pedro being temporarily out of the house over the next two days. Precise descriptions of the two British visitors had been supplied in the event of Pedro being unavailable. Both medium height, the man with dark hair, a serious expression, the woman with wavy, light brown hair; she would probably be the one to attempt to engage in conversation, or some form of communication, given the language barrier. Luisa took a deep breath, calmed herself and opened the door.

Sophie smiled and addressed the lady of the house. *'Bom dia, Senhora Gomes?'*

'Sim,' Luisa replied.

Bear then heard Sophie add an explanation that included the words for English, friend, husband and London. They were both unsure as to how such a garbled message would be received but were surprised and relieved that the lady opened the door wide and gestured for them to enter.

This is proving too easy, Bear thought as he shot a glance

at Sophie, whose shrug and baffled expression indicated that she had a similar impression.

'Please,' Luisa said in broken English, beckoning them to a small sitting room with two armchairs and a sofa. She gestured to her visitors to take a seat and they duly occupied places on the sofa. 'My husband...,' she added, smiling nervously, pointing to her watch, then holding up all fingers of her hands, *'dez minutos.'* She made an additional comment in Portuguese which neither of her visitors understood but which they presumed to be an explanation for Pedro's temporary absence.

There ensued a slightly uncomfortable few minutes as Luisa introduced herself and repeated her visitors' names to ensure correct pronunciation, although she retained a quizzical look on hearing Bear's name. With extensive conversation impossible, she made a remark on the weather. Bear this time understood the word *'frio'*.

'Sim,' he ventured in response, *'Guarda fria e formosa.'* That compliment about the city's beauty drew an amused smile from the hostess, although Sophie looked at her companion in puzzlement as to how he had acquired such a phrase. Brief two- or three-word exchanges peppered what passed for conversation for several minutes, ranging from references to weather in London to a nice painting above a mantelpiece and Lisbon being busy. Luisa seemed relaxed with waiting for her husband to join them, when in reality she was on edge and was earnestly hoping he would reappear before her guests gave up and left.

Finally, a key turned in the lock and a familiar voice was heard from the front door.

Pedro had decided to take himself on a shopping errand

on foot, partly for exercise after being confined to the train for much of the previous day, but also to clear his head prior to the likely arrival of guests. A few quiet words of confirmation from his wife revealed that that moment had arrived. Moments later the antiques dealer stepped into the sitting room. His guests rose to greet him.

'Good morning! Welcome to Guarda,' he greeted them warmly but nervously. 'I somehow thought we would meet again.' He offered his hand, which each of his visitors took firmly. 'Sophia and Ben, if I remember?'

'Sophie, actually,' Sophie corrected him.

'And Bear,' added Bear.

Bear was not in the least surprised to have to repeat his name before it was understood. Pedro turned to his wife to say something in Portuguese. From her smile it was clear that he was supplying the name of a wild animal to denote the unusual moniker, which cleared up Luisa's bewilderment from earlier. Pedro gestured to his guests to take their seats and he sat down in one of the armchairs. Luisa occupied the other; although she could understand very little of the exchanges that ensued, she followed the body language of the visitors studiously, as if to pick up any clues that might be helpful to her husband.

'I hope you had a pleasant journey,' Pedro initiated the conversation awkwardly.

'Yes, thank you,' Sophie replied. 'I suppose you're wondering what brings us here.'

'I did wonder. Perhaps you would like to tell me?'

'Well, maybe we should tell you the whole story. I remember you said you like people to be direct...'

'Before you do,' Pedro broke off to say something to Luisa, who left the room, 'would you like coffee?'

Bear thanked Pedro and assented, and so did Sophie on this occasion, although she rarely drank coffee, so as not to complicate matters by asking for an alternative drink and extend an awkward conversation. But Pedro had carefully prepared his next move.

'I wonder what causes two young people to take time off work in the middle of winter. I mean, people don't come to Guarda for Christmas shopping, not from London, anyway.' He tried to deliver this planned line calmly, but his voice gave away the tension he was experiencing. He was clearly not wholly at ease in his own home.

'I had the week off anyway,' answered Bear, 'I'm a teacher and our holidays started last Friday.'

'And I sell books for a living,' added Sophie. As no immediate comment from their host was forthcoming, she clarified, 'Educational books for schools. I visited Bear's school recently.'

Pedro was not surprised at Sophie's involvement in sales. She had that poise and energy one would expect from someone used to dealing with the public trying to persuade them to part with their cash.

'You work in sales?' asked Pedro. 'Do you have a business card on you? '

'Of course,' Sophie replied, reaching into her handbag for her purse and offered him her card with her qualifications, job title and the address and telephone number of Foundation Books printed on it. Pedro studied the details, headed to a telephone in the corner of the room and dialled. His visitors heard only Pedro's half of the conversation, but it was enough to establish the reason for the call.

'Excuse me, can I speak to Sophie Bingham in the

Education Department, please…? My name is Juan Gomez… Yes, certainly… Thank you… Yes… Oh, is she…? All week? When will she be back…? I'll try on Monday then… No need, I'll ring her on Monday… Thank you… Goodbye.'

Pedro hung up and sat down as his wife re-entered the room with coffee mugs, which she distributed. He apologised for making the call.

'I'm sorry about that, but I had to check up on you. The police have been around twice as they think I might have something to do with some jewel fraud.'

'We know,' said Bear. 'It's been in the papers in England.'

'So at least I know you're not working under cover,' Pedro said to Sophie with an uneasy smile.

'How about me?' Bear challenged him. 'I don't have a card, but I can give you my school's number. It's holiday time, but there should be someone in the office who can vouch for me.'

'That won't be necessary,' said Pedro. 'So you are not in the police. Why are you here?'

'We have something you really wanted,' Sophie resumed. 'We know it's worth much more than you offered for it, and we would like to know why.'

Pedro knew better than to ask if the visitors had brought the brooch with them. Instead he asked, 'How do you know how much it's worth?'

Sophie described their visit to the Instituto de Cultura Nacional and Manuel Cardoso's valuation. Pedro had not met Manuel but had heard the name of the expert. She referred to this mysterious person who lived outside Lisbon who loaned brooches to the National Museum on a regular basis. Pedro did not make any acknowledgement at this point to confirm or deny that he was that person. Bear mentioned his earlier valuation and why they felt they needed to return to Portugal for a more informed opinion. Sophie added the revelation of D'Oliveira's arrest, saying she would like to be sure that Pedro was not involved in any fraud. If he was clean, and the brooch that she owned really did belong with three others, maybe they needed to talk further. She was careful not to disclose any further intentions.

'So you may have the missing piece in the puzzle?' Pedro asked. 'What is it you call it, jigsaw puzzle?'

Sophie nodded. She waited for further comment, then continued. 'If there's anything you can say that can convince us that you have nothing to do with this fraud, perhaps we can come to some arrangement.'

'I can do more than that. I need to show you something,' Pedro replied confidently, the anxiety in his manner lifting. He seemed much more in control of the situation. 'But first, I suggest we finish our coffee. It will take some time to show you properly and when we're finished, the coffee will be cold, I assure you.'

The guests drank up in relative silence and amid some quite incongruous small talk about the paintings and prints decorating the Gomes's sitting room. When it was clear that the hot drinks had been more or less consumed, Pedro rose and invited his visitors to follow him out of the room. Luisa followed behind them.

They passed along a corridor, then turned right into a larger, more spacious lounge which extended to a set of French windows. Even at a cursory glance outside, and despite the wintry season, it was evident that a thoughtfully constructed garden was being maintained with an array of plants and a water feature adorning the centre of the lawn. The area just before the French windows formed an alcove slightly apart from the rest of the lounge and contained some easy chairs to the right. To the left was a more robust chair; on closer inspection it was apparent that it was a wheelchair, occupied by a dark-haired, youthful figure. In front of the wheelchair was a television set that was switched on to an American news channel. As the party of four approached the chair, Pedro called out gently. Bear caught just the word *'Inglaterra'* and realised their host was about to make an introduction. The occupant of the chair swung around, activated the remote control to switch off the television and looked up at the guests, saying, 'Hi guys, how are you doing?'

'Hello,' Bear and Sophie responded in unison.

'Meet Tiago, my son,' Pedro said.

'Hello, Tiago,' said Sophie. Bear added his greeting.

'Tiago has been picking up some English through the news channels. He knows a few phrases, but he can't speak much. We hope he will be able to go to America one day. At the moment he relies on the wheelchair.'

'What's wrong with him?' asked Sophie, turning to Pedro but having difficulty tearing her eyes from something she could see across Tiago's chest.

'Traumatic brain injury,' Pedro explained. 'He was knocked over by a cyclist while he was playing outside when he was two. He hit his head hard on the pavement. We took him to hospital immediately, of course, and for days it was not clear whether he would live. Thankfully, he came through but with severe injuries. His movements are limited because of the brain injuries. He cannot transmit the messages to his limbs to move normally. He also has difficulty in reading. He can only read a few words.'

The visitors looked on the youngster sympathetically. They guessed he must be about nine or ten. He had a slightly faraway look in his eyes and his head was tilted to one side. Pedro put an affirming hand on Tiago's shoulder.

'But he is a bright lad. He can argue about American politics and the environment. The television keeps him informed, but he gets tired easily.' Pedro addressed his son, who clearly needed a translation for any lengthy speech. Tiago smiled and nodded.

'Is he getting any treatment?' asked Bear.

'Some. We have therapists who come in every afternoon and help with his movement. A tutor visits three times a week to help with speech and language and numeracy. But he needs more radical, constant therapy for it to make a difference. At the moment one of us needs to be in the house all the time for him. He's ten now; this has been a way of life for eight years.'

'Can't the state help?' asked Sophie. 'It sounds like there may be a cure available from what you say.'

Pedro sighed, and related to his guests a story he had told many times. Luisa nodded at times, not understanding every word, but clearly so familiar with the details that she was fully aware what her husband was explaining.

'The state can provide limited funding for traumatic brain injury. Once there is no immediate danger to life, they can provide the therapists who work on his movement, with limited success, but that's all.' Pedro paused, as his guests gazed compassionately at Tiago and back to Pedro, sympathising with a seemingly impossible situation. He added, 'But science is improving all the time. There is a centre in Philadelphia that can do some wonderful things, but you have to commit to spending several months there for the experts to assess the child and work on their movement and brain functions daily. They have achieved some great things for children with brain injuries, but it's very expensive. We have saved some money to go there, but we have a long way to go before we can afford such treatment.'

Bear and Sophie were silent for a moment, needing to absorb the enormity of what had just been imparted. Sophie looked again at Tiago and smiled. She asked him how he was in Portuguese, to which he replied, 'Great, ma'am! You bet!' He was clearly delighted to be able to start to show off his repertoire of acquired phrases. Sophie exchanged a thumbs-up with the boy, then looked closer at the objects that had initially attracted her attention. She could not resist the temptation to step closer and inspect. When she was able to distinguish what she was staring at, she let out a gasp.

'Are these three...?' she began, turning to Pedro. 'Exactly,' Pedro replied.

Bear also drew close to Tiago and was able to confirm what his companion had noticed. Tiago was wearing a white sweatshirt, across which a black leather band or belt was attached diagonally. Fastened on to the band were three bronze objects. Each had the design of a horse and rider and the unmistakable Latin motto emblazoned on the front. Bear looked at Pedro, open-mouthed.

'So you have the other three brooches?' Bear asked unnecessarily.

'Let's say, we have been collecting them,' Pedro replied. He gestured to them all to be seated in the lounge and directed Tiago to turn his wheelchair around to join in the gathering, as there was nothing to share that his son did not already know.

The visitors prepared themselves for a long story, but not with any steely determination born from boredom; rather, they were captivated as pieces of the puzzle of the last few months were falling into place. For Pedro and Luisa, the construction of the jigsaw had begun years earlier.

'The first brooch I discovered by chance when clearing my grandmother's house when she died. I thought it was a nice badge, slightly strange picture of a skull in the background. I kept it, but I somehow didn't think an image of death was right to give to my wife.' Pedro translated these thoughts for the benefit of his wife and son, but their quick recognition indicated that they had both heard this clarification before. He continued, 'That was before Tiago was born. Then shortly after his accident, I came across brooch number two at a market. Just like what you said happened at Valença. Couldn't believe my luck. It was so cheap. Just for fun I pinned the two brooches on his little sweater. He had been crying a lot that day, but the brooches seemed to calm him down. From then on, I always kept them near Tiago. If we had to take them away for polishing, he would become unsettled again. Then for number three, about four years ago, I was at an auction and had to outbid someone. I paid more than I should but by now I was convinced they were part of a series. Luisa thought I was mad when I told her how much I had paid.' Again, Pedro translated that part of his story to his wife, who responded with a wry smile.

'By now I knew I needed to get them valued. I had put the three brooches on a band and attached it to Tiago's sweater. He always seemed more at peace when all three were there. I learned about this place in Philadelphia and how we could get treatment that might change Tiago's future. I got the three valued while away in Lisbon for a few days. Apparently, Tiago was really distressed while I was away, not for me, but for the brooches.' He translated again for his son's benefit, asking if the boy remembered, which he did, with a cheeky grin.

'Did you meet Manuel Cardoso?' asked Sophie.

'No, he was away that day. I left them with the National Museum who signed a form to say they had received them and said they'd get back to me. A week later they wrote to me saying Cardoso had inspected the brooches and was convinced they were part of a set. The museum then suggested that I loaned them out to them for display. I said I could only do that for short periods; otherwise Tiago would get really unsettled. It seemed to have a comforting effect whenever the brooches were with him. I was surprised that the museum agreed to have them on display a month at a time, then for two months. That was about as much as Tiago could manage, but as he has grown older, he knows that the museum fees are paying for his treatment, and, we hope, a trip to America.'

'What did the museum say about having the fourth brooch?' asked Bear. 'They must know that there's a fourth brooch somewhere that completes the set.'

'Well…' Pedro paused before replying, 'of course they do. They said that having all four Horsemen of the Apocalypse on display would generate huge interest and they would pay handsomely. The display would attract visitors from around the world, they said. "If you ever find the missing piece, Senhor Gomes, you will be able to stay in America for as long as your son wants."'

'So that's why you were so keen to buy the brooch back in London,' Sophie responded as Pedro fell silent. The dealer nodded, and Sophie shook her head sadly. Bear noticed tears streaming down both her cheeks as she struggled to come to terms with the enormity of the Gomes family's challenge. He felt a lump in his throat too, and for a moment was unsure how to proceed in the conversation. It was Sophie who hesitantly broke the silence. 'This is a silly question, but what would you do with the fourth brooch, the missing piece in the puzzle, if you had it?'

Pedro was slightly taken aback by such a direct question, the answer to which he had already given. He realised that he needed to articulate his plans plainly. He said simply, 'I would contact the National Museum, ask them to get the brooch officially verified and valued by Manuel Cardoso. If it is confirmed as genuine, I would arrange for all four horsemen to be on display at regular intervals of two months at a time. I don't think Tiago could be parted from them for longer. When it was financially sensible, I would make arrangements for us to move to Philadelphia for as long as the treatment takes. Possibly two years, they reckon.'

The dealer fell silent. He had presented his situation as clearly and succinctly as possible. He had the impression that his words had been sifted by a jury as if he were under oath and that he was duty bound to carry out his plans to the letter. He knew that his visitors needed to hear what amounted to a solemn vow. Sophie looked away to the window as though mentally weighing the significance of her host's words. As no immediate reply was forthcoming, Pedro gently asked, 'I think you know that I have to ask you again… how much do you want for the brooch?'

She looked him full in the eye and answered, 'How much does someone's whole future cost?' She reached into her coat pocket that she had carried through from the other sitting room, extracted an envelope and placed a shining bronze object on the coffee table between them. 'This is for Tiago's future. I don't want any money for it. The price is that you carry out your promise and make sure he gets to Philadelphia.'

'Are you sure?' asked Pedro, not daring to believe that his quest of several years was reaching the home straight at last. Bear was about to ask the same question, but he had secretly imagined what he would have done in Sophie's situation, and hoped he would have had the courage to choose exactly the same course of action.

Tiago's eyes lit up as his father inspected the item of jewellery, including the inscription on the back. It was unquestionably of the same design as its three predecessors. Pedro said something to his son, who beamed at Sophie, saying, *'Muito, muito obrigado!* Thank you, thank you!'

'You're welcome,' Sophie replied quietly.

Pedro insisted that the guests stayed for lunch. What had been a sombre moment became one of strange elation as he announced his way forward. That he was confident in each step reflected the fact that he had had four years to decide how to proceed should brooch number four ever come into his possession. He insisted that his visitors witness him writing to the National Museum claiming to have received a generous donation of the missing seventeenth-century horseman brooch and asking for its valuation to be initiated. He included a promise to use proceeds for the long-term therapy needed by his son. He asked if Sophie wished to be acknowledged as the donor, but she declined. The lunch hour proved to be a jovial time, with Pedro translating anecdotes from the past few months to his wife and son. Bear's mysterious conversation with Brian Worthington that was overheard by John Billington drew particularly boisterous laughter from Tiago, who referred to Bear as 'James Bond' thereafter. Bear apologised for his aggressive behaviour in the Camden pub, and Pedro related what a fool he felt following them that afternoon. Luisa was fascinated that the two guests had met only as recently as August, and in her own country as well. If it hadn't rained that day, she reflected to her husband, they would never have seen the brooch.

'It's not that surprising, darling,' joked Pedro 'up there, along the Green Coast line, it always rains. In Guarda, it's always cold.' He was about to translate but both Bear and Sophie indicated they had got the gist of his quip.

The visiting therapists were due to see Tiago in the early afternoon and the 'brooch pair', having delivered their cargo, prepared to leave. They were just able to hug Tiago without him having to adjust his position in the wheelchair, then were embraced by Luisa and, finally, Pedro.

'Thank you both for your gift. To say "thank you" is so inadequate. For the first time in years I feel a peace in my heart that has been missing for so long,' he confessed.

'In a funny way, although it hasn't been anything like as long, we feel that too,' replied Sophie, looking at Bear for assent, which was freely given.

The visitors took their leave and headed back to the old town, for no particular reason other than that was the district with which they were familiar. They realised their journey had reached its meaningful, although unexpected conclusion. Inevitably, after some moments of silence, Sophie asked, 'Do you think I did the right thing? I mean, what if Pedro…?'

'It doesn't matter what he does,' interrupted Bear, 'either way, you did the right thing. If you had done anything else, you would have regretted it for a long time.'

After a soul-searching morning, Bear proposed some sightseeing for the rest of the afternoon with the cathedral and other historic buildings on the agenda. The following day, they took their leave of Guarda, both resolving to return one day in the summer, if only to prove Pedro's assertion about the climate to be wrong. The following day saw them return to Lisbon, and the train journey was enlivened at several points by the script of 'The Joy of Four'. Sophie agreed to act out the parts of other characters in Cynthia's play while Bear tried to memorise his lines with only occasional reminders from his prompter. On the Friday after an uneventful flight they were back at Sophie's flat in Camden and Bear prepared to head back to Suffolk.

Sophie invited Bear in for a cup of tea. He insisted he wouldn't stay long as he wanted to beat the rush hour traffic (it was early afternoon by then). Of course, she was profuse in her gratitude in accompanying her on their trip. Bear had queried this view, fearful that his presence had persuaded her to part with an item of jewellery that she could have sold on for a handsome profit. Sophie found it hard to articulate how she felt, except that she had experienced a sense of completion at resolving the mystery of the brooch. Perhaps she knew there was always a fourth person in the drama, she added, in reference to Tiago. Bear drank up and prepared to head outside to his car for the final leg of his journey. He was about to repeat the half-hearted closing greeting he had uttered in October, when it had seemed that the brooch affair was closed, only for it to reopen again. This time he found it still harder to part. They exchanged the inevitable 'If you're in the area…' remarks, but both felt flat at the parting. Bear asked himself:

do I feel more than just friendship, a warm companionship and an amusing complicity with this person that brought about an unusual adventure? He certainly hoped to see her again but reasoned quickly that she was just someone whom he admired, who had certainly taken the lead more and more, especially in the two days in Guarda. Yet she demonstrated few signs of sharing the same fundamental beliefs or views of the world, having shown only a curious interest in the conversation about the number four in Manuel's office. Should they attempt to see each other again? They hugged warmly and wished each other a happy Christmas and Bear drove away, confused. His travelling companion was similarly preoccupied that evening.

＊

Chapter Eighteen
The Joy of Four

Grove Street Baptist Church was located on one of the streets off the main thoroughfare, about five minutes' walk from the centre of Princewood. A modern building, constructed in the 1970s, it was designed to accommodate a congregation of some two hundred worshippers and enjoyed a regular attendance of about half as many for a Sunday service. On this last Sunday afternoon before Christmas, however, numbers had swelled with invitations to Cynthia's spectacular having been issued and met with a positive response. The church did look impressive with a distinct festive feel to the surroundings. The Christmas tree in the corner was amply decorated and a beautifully constructed nativity scene had been installed near the front, next to a ring of four advent candles. As this was the fourth and last Sunday in Advent, the final candle had been ceremoniously lit and there was a discernible aura and buzz about the place to indicate that a significant season had almost arrived. Perhaps the enigmatic title of Cynthia's production had helped, or her enthusiastic marketing of the event, but there was a higher than usual anticipation in the air, noticeable in various conversations, that Christmas would be truly ushered in with the performance about to unfold.

Bear allowed himself a furtive look through a tiny gap between curtains on the makeshift stage. It was clear that with

225

still ten minutes until curtain up, the church was filling up nicely. He berated himself with a tinge of regret that he had not made more of an effort in inviting people. There had been Sophie, of course, with a crumpled ticket on the train to Guarda. Otherwise he had made a passing reference to acting in a nativity play to a colleague he had bumped into in town the day before, effectively saying that he was welcome to watch if he was at a loose hand. The half-hearted invitation had been acknowledged politely with a non-committal response. Bear had the excuse of being abroad for most of the past week, but he knew he could have shown more commitment in publicising the event. He remembered two years ago managing to persuade Rob to attend a carol service, and subsequent attempts to engage his friend on matters spiritual had been met with a defensive but adroit resistance as if to say, 'You have your beliefs; I have mine'. That was fair enough, thought Bear, although Rob had never really articulated what his views were. Nor had Sophie, for that matter, except that her questions and observations surrounding Manuel's explanations displayed more than simply polite curiosity.

A tap on the elbow from a fellow cast member reminded Bear that it was time to clear the wings in readiness for the first scene. A few minutes later the actors could hear a youthful voice singing the first verse of 'Once in Royal David's City' indicating the formal beginning of the afternoon's proceedings. The congregation then rose to their feet to join in the rest of the verses. As they sat down, a narrator, usually known as Chris Hepton, solicitor in working hours but masquerading as a shepherd, took to the stage. In his best manufactured agricultural accent, he welcomed them all to

Judea and told them he had been labouring in these hills all his life, man and boy, tending the sheep and keeping the wolves at bay. He wanted to tell them a strange but wonderful story that happened in these parts many years ago and invited everyone, young and old, to join in as they relived an amazing adventure.

The show progressed with the familiar plot of the nativity interspersed with well-known carols. The timing of the carols (and hence the opportunity for audience participation) had been adeptly blended into the narrative by Cynthia. As Joseph and Mary wearily approached Bethlehem, mentioning the reason for their journey being to comply with Roman census regulations, Joseph pointedly remarked that they had reached the little town of Bethlehem. That was the trigger for the audience to stand and sing, with encouraging gesticulation from the shepherd-narrator, led by a music group with brass, strings and percussion all prominent. Shortly afterwards 'Angels from the Realms of Glory' was given an obvious cue from one of the shepherds pointing skywards, and the narrator was in fine form directing the congregation to extend the vowel sound on 'Cooooome and worship' to the full in the chorus.

Cynthia knew just how much pantomime and farce to inject without being irreverent. A conversation was struck up between an older and younger shepherd, during which they commented on the cold night air. The older shepherd reminisced of special nights in the past, of great feast days, and recalled 'Good King Wenceslas' on the feast of Stephen. That, the audience by now grasped, was a cue for the carol of that name. Quick reference to the carol sheets informed the gathering of division between male and female parts to mirror the roles of king and page. The obvious blatant anachronism was not lost on the audience, nor the younger shepherd whose next line after the carol was, 'But Wenceslas hasn't even been born yet.'

'Never let trivial details get in the way of a good story, lad,' replied the older colleague, 'as your grandad used to say, truth is timeless.' Amazing, mused Bear from the wings, only Cynthia could pull such tricks off.

Bear's first appearance on stage provoked admiring gasps at the intricate decorations of the costumes that he and his fellow wise men wore. Three colourful gowns, in Bear's case, dark green, with silver, glistening trimmings and a prominent turban with crown attached on each of their heads. They acted out the scene where they were met by Herod, who was greeted with good-natured pantomime boos and hisses. Stephanie's comic slip in interpreting unnecessarily was beautifully timed and elicited hearty laughter. Bear's second contribution came as the magi approached the manger with gifts to present, each carefully wrapped with ribbon.

'And who are you when you're at home?' asked Joseph of the three foreign visitors.

'We are not at home. We have travelled from distant lands,' explained Bear, alias Melchior.

'We are three wise men. Some people call us kings in our own country,' added Balthazar.

'But we have come to worship a fourth king who is greater than us,' continued Gaspar, 'we know we could not be at peace until we met him.'

In those few seconds, the memory of meeting Tiago and the sense of completeness struck Bear like a light bulb coming on. The missing fourth person, with potential to be fulfilled many years into the future. The comparisons were striking. He wished Sophie could be present to witness such a visual demonstration of a concept that had stirred her curiosity. He did not have time to dwell on such reflections as Joseph was about to deliver his next cue.

'So where are you from?' Joseph questioned them further.

'We come from the East, the distant orient,' answered Bear. 'Let me explain…'

At these words, the shepherd-narrator gestured to the audience to stand again, although by now most had grasped the pattern of proceedings and were already on their feet to join in the next carol. The whole building resounded to the first verse of 'We Three Kings of Orient Are', followed by the chorus. The congregation fell silent as first Nigel Burrows delivered Gaspar's verse about his gift of gold, followed by Bear's rendition of Melchior's offering of frankincense and John Compton, alias Balthazar, singing of myrrh. Each king followed his verse with a reverent bow to the infant Jesus, hidden away in various cloths in Mary's arms, and presentation of his gift with a flourish. Bear was relieved to have belted out his solo relatively clearly and without hesitation; it had been the part he had most been dreading. The carol was concluded with a rousing final verse and chorus in which all participated. Suitably invigorated, the audience took their seats as the play resumed.

The remainder of the performance was completed virtually seamlessly. Cynthia had been astute enough to reserve 'Away in a Manger' for a children's choir, thus guaranteeing attendance of parents and grandparents. Further dialogue paved the way for 'Ding Dong Merrily on High' with the narrator telling the audience that the extended vowel in the earlier carol had just been a warm-up, and they should really

229

raise the roof with 'Gloooria' in the ensuing chorus. The vocal cords took a hammering, and what was lacking in harmony was certainly compensated for by enthusiasm. As seats were resumed, the narrator summed up the afternoon in verse that wished them all much festive cheer. Just as the three kings were looking for the missing fourth king, the trio of Father, Son and Spirit were looking for a fourth person to relate to, particularly at this special time of year. After a slight deliberate pause, the narrator thanked the audience for coming and led the cast in a curtain call and a presentation of flowers to the spectacular's director, to rapturous applause.

As Michael Standish eased his way to the front, Bear anxiously muttered to himself, suppressing his wish that the minister did not go over the top. Sometimes he could not resist the temptation to unleash his evangelistic zeal and was liable, for all good intentions, to put guests off who were unfamiliar with such a setting and message. Bear need not have worried. Michael was not about to steal his wife's thunder. Four was a great number, he said; four gospels told us how the story continued, and free copies were available to any interested enquirers at the back. He announced that all were welcome at the Christmas Day service and he hoped to see many on that occasion. He concluded by wishing all a happy Christmas and encouraging everyone to stay for refreshments, not that much encouragement was needed.

As he made his way to the serving hatch at the back of the auditorium in pursuit of a well-deserved glass of mulled wine and mince pie, Bear's attention was drawn to an elderly lady, Margaret Philips, stalwart of the congregation, who was in conversation with a younger woman. He did not need a second glance to identify the latter.

'There he is! Here comes a wise man!' Margaret exclaimed as Bear approached with an amused grin.

'You made it!' Bear remarked appreciatively.

'Well, I had to make an effort,' Sophie replied as Margaret eased herself away, making her excuses. 'To be honest, it was a last-minute decision. A combination of riding not being possible because of the frost making the ground too hard, and … I don't know, I was sort of intrigued. I couldn't get the number four out of my head.'

'I've got to be honest, too,' Bear confessed sheepishly, 'I was rather half-hearted in giving out the invitation.'

'I know. But I'm glad you did. It's been… interesting. You did well, by the way. Loved the solo.'

'Thanks. And thanks for coming all this way. In what way interesting?'

'Well, I never imagined church was so… well, wacky and fun, almost. I imagined it to be… well, sort of sombre and serious.'

'It can be both… serious and fun, I mean, sometimes at the same time. But it's been fun today.'

Bear accompanied Sophie to the hatch for refreshments. She declined the mulled wine in favour of a cup of tea as she had to drive back, but he was grateful for a glass after the stress of the performance. Amid a few pats on the back and expressions of 'Well done, wise man', Bear asked her if she had recovered from their adventure.

'Just about, although I did wake up yesterday wondering how it had all happened.'

'No regrets about your decision with the brooch?' Bear asked cautiously.

'I just felt that there would be a fourth person all along,

231

and meeting Tiago sealed it. I just knew I had to help. Thank you so much for coming with me.'

'For what?' Bear jested. 'If it hadn't been for me, you would be a whole lot richer.'

'If it hadn't been for you, I would never have known… Oh, you know,' she said with a shrug. He did know; they had performed this ritual of mutual regret and apology more than once over the past few months. 'I'm just excited to see how the future shapes up for Tiago in the years ahead. I hope somehow we can keep in touch with Pedro and Luisa.'

'Talking of how the future shapes up,' Bear said, swiftly walking over to a display table and removing a paperback book. On an impulse he took a copy of Luke's gospel and handed it to Sophie. 'If you're interested in how this afternoon's story continues, it's all in here. If you have a spare hour or so over Christmas. You may have some idea of how it ends, but the middle bits are worth reading and thinking about.' He was unsure how this offer might be received and was relieved that it was accepted warmly.

'Thank you, Bear, I will have a read sometime,' Sophie replied.

They shared observations about their trip and repeated their determination to revisit Guarda one day when it was warmer and were still chatting while the gathering had thinned out. Church secretary Anne Broadbent was busying herself taking photographs of the social interaction over refreshments to complement others taken during the spectacle. Bear realised he was still in his costume and was about to make moves to remove it when Sophie remarked at the Christmas decorations. Her attention was then drawn to the main exit door at what appeared to be leaves dangling from just above the door frame.

'Ah, the mistletoe,' she remarked. 'That's something I've never done before.'

Bear looked at her, momentarily baffled before responding with a smile, which was abruptly misinterpreted by the watching church secretary.

'Oh yes, you must!' Anne Broadbent, who had obviously been overhearing, exclaimed enthusiastically. 'Come on, you two, that would make a great picture!'

'Come on, Bear,' said Sophie, leading him by the hand to a position facing the photographer underneath the symbolic plant. She then theatrically planted a solid kiss on his cheek while Anne photographed, saying triumphantly, 'I've never kissed a wise man before.'

'How do you know you still haven't?' Bear responded with a chuckle. 'Just so you definitely come away from Princewood with a first, I'm sure you've never had a Christmas kiss from a bear before.'

Bear duly provided the reciprocal salute that was captured by Anne, who thanked them both for being such good sports.

'It's all right for you, I've got to live here. You can escape back to London!' Bear commented with a hearty laugh, pointing a mock-accusatory finger in Sophie's direction. 'You should have heard the gossip that Friday night when you visited the school, and now there will be photos all over the church magazine. People will talk!'

'The price of fame, Bear,' said Sophie, 'that comes with the territory of being a wise man.'

They had enjoyed a laugh together and the shared experience clearly enabled them to relax in each other's company. The building was emptying now, and Sophie said she really needed to make tracks back to the capital, but she had enjoyed the afternoon that had given her 'much to think about'. She was, indeed, in thoughtful mode once more. Bear considered briefly whether to invite Sophie back to his flat for further refreshment, but she seemed determined to beat the weekend traffic before returning to work the following day. He was not sure whether to be disappointed at not pursuing the conversation further but felt curiously relaxed not to feel the need to risk imposing himself on her.

'Do you think it was fate that we met back in August?' she asked Bear.

Bear was tempted to respond with a cryptic phrase such as 'God works in mysterious ways' but restrained himself. He had no way of being certain that Divine will had directed their paths. He had simply felt an inner compulsion to see this adventure through to its conclusion, one that had been given impetus by his passion for borders. His response was simple and heartfelt.

'All I know is that we met because we decided to cross the same border on the same day, on a wet day when it would have been easier to have stayed at home. Because of that a ten-year-old's life may be changed for ever.'

'What a crazy game life is sometimes!' reflected Sophie. 'Wasn't there once some wacky TV game show called *Jeux sans frontières*, games without borders?'

'There was,' recalled Bear, 'I can just about remember. It was a lot of fun for a few years.'

'Well, if each time we cross a border, we can do some good and change someone's life even a little, it's got to be worth it, don't you think?' Sophie wondered, smiling inquisitively at Bear, who nodded in assent. 'Cross borders, build bridges,' she added, 'how's that for a slogan for the new year?'

As they went their separate ways that evening, it was a motto that took deep root in Bear over the ensuing holidays, and his thoughts turned intermittently to the afternoon in Valença do Minho. He was sure that Gustave Eiffel and his contemporaries would approve.

Printed in Great Britain
by Amazon

63373865R00139